JN302480

「少年T」の
ヒロシマ
いま伝えたい真実の叫び！

田邊雅章

〝原爆の子〟から映像作家へ

第三文明社

"人の一生は、宿命から逃れることはできない、ならば、いかに受け入れるかである"

――著者

はじめに

一九四五年（昭和二十年）八月六日。廣島に人類史上初めての原子爆弾が投下された。

そのとき、私は国民学校の二年生、八歳だった。

私の生家は、現在の「原爆ドーム」（当時は「広島県産業奨励館」）の東隣りにあった。原爆により、両親と弟が生命を奪われた。私自身も二日後の八月八日、爆心地とも知らず変わり果てた生家跡に戻り、三日間にわたって市内中心部の被災者収容施設を訪ね歩き家族を捜し求めた。その結果、残留放射能を浴びて「入市被爆者」となった。

残された家族は年老いた祖母だけ。それからの日々、苛酷で悲惨な生活を強いられ、身体は原因不明の発熱、下痢、けだるさ、原爆後遺症特有の症状に苦しめられた。

あまりの苦しさから、祖母は「みんなが待つ、あの世に行こうか」と

つぶやくこともあった。子ども心にも、それが何を意味するかはわかっていた。

その祖母も原爆後遺症と被爆後の生活苦が災いして九年後に他界。私は文字通り「ひとりぼっち」天涯孤独の身となった。

少年時代から私は自身に言い聞かせてきた。

「原爆のことは忘れよう」

「不運を恨んでもしかたがない、自力で生き延びるために、あらゆる努力をしてみよう」

それは仏教でいう「諦観（ていかん）」の思想に近かったのかもしれない。悟りとまではゆかないまでも、心の支えを必要とした。

成人後、映像作家として活動をしてきたのだが、意識的に「原爆」に関与する仕事は避けている自分がいた。頑なに原爆体験へ背を向けるかのような生き方だった。

しかし、還暦を迎えたとき人生の大きな転機が訪れた。それは、爆心地復元事業として被爆前の町を映像によって再現する仕事に着手したこ

である。まさしく被爆者であり、映像作家である私にしかできない仕事だった。爆心地に生まれ育ち、被爆者としての宿命を背負って生きてきた自分が、後世に「映像」をもって原爆の実相を伝えることは、自分にとっての使命でもあると思えるようになったのだ。

自らが被爆者でありながら、それをひた隠すような生き方をしてきたのだが、あの日亡くなった多くの犠牲者の無念さ、人類史上類を見ない悲惨な原爆の実態を、「映像」をもって訴えていくという作業を通じて、残された人生を全力で、原爆と真正面から対峙するという決意にいたった。

一九九六年、「原爆ドーム」が世界遺産に登録された。それをきっかけに、被爆以前の「広島県産業奨励館」時代の姿と、それをとりまく伝統的な街並みや生活文化を、映像でよみがえらせるプロジェクトを立ち上げた。爆心地をよみがえらせる初めての仕事だけに、国内はもとより海外からも注目され、二〇〇〇年には爆心地復元シリーズの第一作『原爆ドームと消えた街並み』をニューヨークの国連本部で上映した。証言をもとにCG画像を駆使した被爆前の街並み、そこに生きる人たちの生活が実

感できる映像であった。

その後、国連本部をはじめ、世界の各地において作品を上映しつつ、原爆の真実について、多くの人々に伝える活動をしてきた。

そうした過程において強く感じたことは、世界の人々が原爆の実態をあまりにも知らないという事実に尽きる。それは、「広島平和記念公園」、その場所は、広島市有数の繁華街であり、原爆投下の瞬間まで多くの人々が生活をしていた場所なのだ。しかし、被爆後につくられたことを知らず、爆心地が公園であったために、原爆の被害は少なくてすんだ部分があると発言したアメリカ人ジャーナリストもいたほどだ。

映像作家として、映像を通じて「原爆」の真実を伝えることとともに、どうしても語り継いでおきたいことがある。被爆者の一人として、その体験を世界に発信する活動を展開してきたからこそ感じることも多い。

そして、少年だった私が体験した「原爆」、自分の目で実際に見たもの、忘れることが出来ない真実を「一次情報」として残しておきたい。

伝えなければならないことは、「原爆」が奪ったものの大きさである。

現状では、世界の多くの人々が、その概略を大まかにとらえているのみである。核兵器としての原爆が、どう爆発し、どれだけの破壊力をもったのか、そういった規模情報を漠然と把握しているだけなのだ。大切なことは、原爆が投下されたその地表に人々が生きていた事実、日常の生活が存在した事実である。

すでに原爆投下から六十七年という歳月が経過した。この半世紀を超える時間は、被爆者の高齢化とともに原爆体験をも風化させつつある。いまこそ、「原爆の真実」を語らなければならないと思う。

それが自分の使命であると強く感じている。

そうした思いから本書の執筆にあたった。

二〇一一年六月。著述に着手し、体験と実証をもとに書き上げたのが本書である。

前述した米国人ジャーナリストもそうであるが、「原爆の実態」について、世界の人々に知ってもらうことが何より大切である。被爆以前と被爆後、その対比において、そうした一次情報を世界に向けて発信する活

動は、これまでほとんどされてこなかった。

一般的に、日本国内においても被爆体験を語ることは、さまざまな場で可能であろうし、また、なされてもきた。

しかしながら、爆心地には何があったのか、どんな町があり、どんな生活があったのか、このことは長年にわたって不明とされてきた。この空白を埋めないで、あの世へゆくことはできない。これは生き残った者の責務である。

本書には、これまで手掛けた記録映画『爆心地復元シリーズ』の画像をはじめ、多くの未公開映像を含む写真を掲載した。ご協力頂いた関係各位や団体機関には、心より感謝の意を表したい。

日本語とともに英訳された本書を、多くの皆さんが手にとって頂けることを強く願っている。とりわけ、次代を担う若い層に読んで頂けるならば、ひときわ嬉しいことでもある。

二〇一二年一月

著　者

「少年T」のヒロシマ　目次

はじめに

第一章　広島の終焉……………13
　一九四五年夏
　母と永遠の別れ
　悲劇の閃光
　この世の地獄
　父は生きていた
　二匹の蛍
　八月十五日──父の最期

第二章 被爆からいかに生きるか……51

占領されたヒロシマ
戦後「ヒロシマ」の真実
運命との出会い
映像ジャーナリストの世界へ
映像作家への道

第三章 運命を生きる──廣島復元事業への決意……85

海外で知った私の中の「ヒロシマ」
ピースサインの女子高生
在りし日の「ふるさと」を探す
「ヒロシマ」を携え国連本部へ

第四章 ヒロシマからのメッセージ〜次の世代への伝承〜

　平和を願う世界の人々へ——遺言
　ヒロシマとフクシマ
　被爆から七十年へ——新たなる決意
　静かに届ける平和の心
　エジプトでの訴え
　私の願う「平和」

あとがき
追記

【凡例】

一、本書における「広島」の表記については、著者の意向により、一般固有名詞としての「広島」、被爆以前の独自の歴史と文化を有した「廣島」、そして被爆後の平和の象徴たる国際都市としての「ヒロシマ」の三種類を使い分けている

一、著者「田邊雅章」の「田邊」姓については、映像作家としての名称であり、本文中の幼少期については「田邉」で表記している

装幀／カズクリエイティブ
本文レイアウト／安藤聡

第一章　廣島の終焉

一九四五年夏

　昭和二十年――。

　戦争はすでに日本の敗色が濃厚になっていたが、国民のどれほどがそのことに気づいていたのだろうか。

　私は当時、現在の小学校にあたる国民学校の二年生（八歳）だった。生家は「広島県産業奨励館」の東隣り。産業奨励館とは、今でいう「原爆ドーム」――つまり爆心地に他ならない。

　父は陸軍将校であったが、家では戦争のことはあまり口にしなかった。父は身の丈六尺を超える偉丈夫で、軍服がよく似合っていた。毎朝当番兵に迎えられ、軍馬にまたがり、腰にサーベルを吊るして陸軍の第五師団司令部に向かう。凛々（りり）しい姿を見るにつけ、大人になったら父のようになりたい――子ども心にそう思っていた。

　当時、父は三十八歳で母は三十二歳。今の私は、もはやその時の両親

ありし日の産業奨励館、右手に筆者の屋敷と土蔵

の倍以上の年齢を生きてしまったが、私の中の父母の面影は、今もその当時のままだ。

当時、国民学校の三年生以上は、すでに県北の学校や寺に集団疎開していた。学校の校庭にたたずむ「勤勉」の象徴、二宮金次郎の銅像は兵器の原料として供出され、プールは防火用水の貯水所となり泳ぐことはできない。

給食のご飯は雑穀交じりで、味噌汁もわずかに野菜が浮かぶ薄い味のものだった。学校も爆撃目標になる恐れがあるとして「家庭学級」という制度がとられていた。近くに生徒を集めて、先生がその家に出向いて午前中だけ簡単な授業をした。私の家でやったこともあるが、教科書を読み、絵日記を見せ合う程度のことで、ほとんど勉強らしい勉強をした覚えがない。

やがて夏休みが始まると、毎日、近所の友だちと連れだって遊んでいた。セミ取りや産業奨励館でのかくれんぼ、庭では陣取り合戦、元安川での水遊び——。食事と昼寝以外は、日中の大半を屋外で過ごしていた。

16

七月の末のことであったと思う。父は、家族全員を母の郷里へ疎開させた。

この時、父は、家のお手伝いさん二人も里帰りさせている。三月十日には、東京大空襲があり十万人以上が亡くなっている。五月二十五日には東京山の手、二十九日には横浜、そして六月には大阪と神戸が襲われた。

六月下旬から、空襲の対象は地方の中小都市に広がっていった。廣島は当時、第五軍司令部、廣島連隊区司令部、中国憲兵隊司令部がおかれる中枢軍都であるにもかかわらず、なぜか大規模な空襲がほとんどなかった。当時の市民にどの程度、被害の深刻さが伝わっていたのか定かではないが、父には何か心にかかるところがあったのだろう。

母と永遠の別れ

疎開先は、廣島から西へ六十キロ離れた山口県の周南市（現・地名）で

17　第一章　廣島の終焉

あった。当時は「熊毛郡高水村」といい、本州では唯一、野生のなべ鶴が渡来する八代盆地南麓の山村である。母と私と一歳の弟、そして祖母の家族四人で、汽車に揺られて岩徳線の高水駅に降り立った。

母方の祖父は、私立高水中学の校長を務めており、伯父は教頭であった。現在の「高水学園」にその名が残っているが、高水中学は、もとは明治三十一年、儒教精神に基づく私塾「高水村塾」として始まっている。創始者は私の曾祖父にあたる宮川泰である。

疎開先は教育者の家だけに、朝から晩まで勉強をさせられるのではないかと心配していたものの、そのそぶりはほとんどない。たまに畑仕事の手伝いや庭の掃除、風呂への水運び、近所へのお使い。それ以外は、すべて遊びで時を過ごした。近くの農家の子どもも加わって、かくれんぼや缶けり、鬼ごっこ、木登り、水遊び、魚釣り、虫とり——。気温が上がる午後には、風通しの良い座敷や日陰の縁側で昼寝をした。日が暮れると、従兄弟たちと怪談話で盛りあがる。さながら林間学校のようでとても楽しかった。

大家族での食事はひときわ賑わう。農村とはいえ、食糧事情は決して良くはなかった。朝食は茶粥に梅干しと塩こぶ。夕飯は芋粥に野菜の煮しめ、沢庵や白菜の漬物、たまに干し魚や鶏肉の切れ端。そんな中で、畑から取れたてのトマトやキュウリは、ほんとうに美味しかった。
「欲しがりません、勝つまでは、お国のために我慢しよう──。」
当時の日本人が皆そうであったように、戦時下の合言葉を唱えながら粗食に耐えた。おやつの蒸かし芋やトウモロコシは嬉

疎開先の屋敷

しかった。廣島と違って甘いお菓子の類はまったくなかった。

八月三日のことだった。高水に来たばかりだというのに、母が弟を連れて廣島に帰るという。お手伝いもおらず、ただひとり残った父の身の周りが心配になったにちがいない。

「すぐ戻ってくるからね——。」

母のその言葉に、「一緒に帰る」と泣いて頼んだが受け入れられなかった。腕白ざかりの私と乳飲み子の弟を連れての廣島行きは、確かにしんどかったのだと思う。

廣島に旅立つ前の晩、母と一緒に風呂に入り身体を流してもらった。

「おじいさまやみんなの言うことをよく聞いて、おとなしくしているのよ。六日には帰ってくるからね——。」

私は大きくうなずいた。しかし、言葉にこそしなかったが、幼心にも妙な胸騒ぎがしていた。不吉な予感だった。そしてこの優しい言葉が、私が聞いた母の最後の言葉になった。

翌朝、私がまだ寝ている間に、母は弟を連れて一番列車で廣島へ発っ

20

母の帰りを待つ時間は長かった。

昼間は、遊んで気を紛らわせることができた。しかし、渓流に河鹿(かじか)蛙(がえる)が姿を見せ、ひぐらしが鳴き渡る夕暮れともなると不安が高まっていく。

不気味な梟(ふくろう)の声がする夜ともなると、いよいよたまらなく寂しくなった。蚊(か)帳(や)の中の祖母に気分転換のお伽(とぎ)噺(ばなし)をねだったのを覚えている。

そして八月六日の朝。空は晴れ渡り雲ひとつなかった。今日は母が帰る日だ。待ち遠しくて仕方がない。

母が帰ってくるのは昼だろうか、それとも夕方だろうか。朝食を終えると祖父と伯父は書類や弁当包みを抱えて学校へ行った。従兄弟たちと木登りをするが、少し風邪気味のせいか、いつものように楽しめなかった。

石段脇の石塀の上に座り、何気なく東の方向を見たときだった。掘割の間で何かが光った。そして次の瞬間「ズン」と、かすかな地響きを感

じた。何が起きたのか――。
他の子どもたちは、みな木登りに熱中しており気にも留めていない。近くの岩国や下松、徳山などでも頻繁に爆撃があったから慣れていたのだろう。

――以下は、後年、私がさまざまな人々から聞いた証言である。

悲劇の閃光（せんこう）

その日、廣島はいつも通りの朝を迎えていたという。
前日の八月五日夜、廣島の東南三十キロにある呉市が空襲を受けていた。廣島市も夜間を通じて空襲警報が発令され、市民の多くは防空壕（ごう）などで暑く眠れぬ夜を過ごした。警報が解除されたのは明け方だったという。子どもから年寄りまで、人々はようやく不安から解放されていた。
空は雲ひとつない快晴である。
その日は月曜日であった。

戦時体制の「国民総動員や勤労奉仕」の美名のもと、働ける者はみな朝早くから仕事場へ出かけていた。徴用工や学徒動員された若者たちもいた。中学生や女学生は軍需工場での手伝いや郵便局での仕分けや配達、土木作業、建物疎開へと動員されていた。

建物疎開とは、家族疎開などで空き家となった家屋を軍の命令で強制的に取り壊す作業をいう。爆撃の火災からの延焼を防ぐためであった。木造家屋の主柱を大人たちが鋸(のこぎり)

爆撃に備えて消火訓練。猿楽町婦人会

で切れ目を入れ、梁に縄やロープをかけて学童たちが力いっぱい引き倒す——今では考えられない原始的な作業が、その頃は随所で当たり前のように行われていた。

家に残るのは子どもや主婦、年寄り、病人などであった。それぞれにいつもと同じ真夏の朝を迎えていたはずである。

子どもたちは朝の涼しいうちに夏休みの宿題帳を広げ、屋外では盥に水を張って水遊び、そして近くの川に出かけて水泳や魚とり。女の子は木陰でお手玉遊びや人形の着せ替え、折り紙などに興じていた。あるいは寺院の境内や墓地ではかくれんぼ、空き地では缶けりや三角ベース（野球の縮小型）もしていたという。

主婦たちは朝の片付けをする時間であった。幼な子を背中におぶって台所の流しで食器を洗う。井戸端では洗濯、部屋や風呂場の掃除、物干しでは洗濯物や布団を広げていた。戦時下とあって防空演習に駆り出され、モンペ姿でバケツリレーの訓練に励む主婦もいた。実戦訓練では、藁人形を敵兵に見立て「エイ、ヤー」との掛け声もろとも竹槍で突き刺

年寄りは行水を使い、あるいは庭木へ水をやり、縁側では縫い物や幼児の子守り、仏壇へのお参り、なかには茶道や華道の稽古ごとや謡曲の練習……。いずれも、のどかな夏の朝である。

　耳を澄ましたなら、廣島の上空へと近づく原爆搭載爆撃機「B29、エノラゲイ」の爆音が聞こえていたかもしれない。

　あの時、私が東の方向に見た光は、原子爆弾の閃光であった。

　そしてまさにその時、高水のはるか東の廣島では、人類史上未曾有の惨状が、この世の地獄が現出していたのである。

　母は弟をおぶったまま土蔵造りの家屋の下敷きに。台所の流しあたりで、ほどなくして想像を絶する灼熱が二人を襲った。弟は生まれたばかりで、人間としての営みを何ら体験しないまま……。

この世の地獄

その日、高水は、午後から急にあわただしくなった。祖父が汗を拭きながら学校から戻ってきた。
「廣島が大変なことになったらしい。田邉（父）は大丈夫だろうか、八重子(えこ)（母）は今日帰ってくる筈だが……。」
祖母と心配そうに話し込んでいたが、私たち子どもには何も教えてくれなかった。ラジオも山間のためか雑音だらけで一向に聞き取れない。祖母は気丈にふるまっていたが内心は不安で不安でたまらなかったに違いない。
「早い時間の汽車に乗っていてくれたら──！」
祖父は神棚へ向かって一生懸命に手を合わせていた。榊(さかき)のそばでは灯明がゆれている。夕食もそこそこに伯父や伯母、近所の人々が集まり何かを話し合っている。

当時は、村役場、郵便局や学校にしかない電話を何度も確認しにいくが広島への電話は一向につながらない。駅に迎えを出し、皆で母の帰りを待ったが、とうとう終列車にも乗っていなかった。

その頃、広島では、夕闇とともに随所に火炎が広がっていた。断末魔の呻き声をあげ、救いを求めるおびただしい被爆者たちが彷徨し、親を探す子どもの叫び声や泣き声、焼け落ちた瓦礫の間からは犠牲者の燐火が飛び交い、さながら阿鼻叫喚の地獄図であったという。

翌日七日も早朝から重い空気があたりを押しつぶしていた。もちろん遊ぶ気にもなれずに一日数本の汽車をただ待ち続けた。前日、閃光を見た石の塀から遥か眼下に岩徳線の線路が見渡たせた。汽笛が聞こえるたび塀に上がって母の帰りを待った。ただひたすらに待った。

午後になって、母の兄姉の伯父と伯母が広島へ捜索に向かった。父母から連絡があった場合にそなえ祖母と私は留まることにした。ほんとうに長い一日だった。日が暮れて涼風に揺れる蚊帳の中、田んぼに舞う蛍を眺めながら不安を打ち消す、それがやっとであった。裏手の森からは

27　第一章　廣島の終焉

狐か狸の鳴き声が聞こえてくる。薄気味悪く不吉な声であった。

「明日こそきっと帰ってくる――。」

その夜、広島の方から帰ってきた村人は言った。

「広島に新型爆弾が落とされ、市内は全滅して一面焼け野原になっていた。生きている人はほとんどいない――。」

待ちきれず、祖母は私を連れて翌朝の一番列車で広島に行くことにした。当時の常備薬である富山の置き薬、着替えや乾パンを祖母とともにズックのずた袋に詰めた。

翌八日の早朝、岩徳線で高水を出発した。岩国から山陽本線へ乗り継いだが広島方面からの列車の乗客の姿は異様なものだった。頭に血まみれの包帯を巻いた人、皮膚は赤黒くひどいやけどを負った人々……。ホーム越しにも目につくのは負傷者の姿ばかりだ。途中駅で異常に待たされ通常の倍以上の時間がかかったと思う。

昼過ぎにようやく己斐（現・西広島）駅に着いた。駅舎を出て私たちは息を飲んだ。

原爆投下直後のきのこ雲

第一章　廣島の終焉

祖母は私が離れないように強く手を握り締める。

数日前に見た「廣島」は魔法のように消え失せていた。街はそのほとんどが焼け落ち、まったく原型を留めていない。今までは建物が遮り、見えるはずのない比治山や黄金山、金輪島、似島がすぐ近くに見える。ポツン、ポツンといくつかの鉄筋建てのビルが僅かに原形をとどめていた。焼け焦げた悪臭、目を覆う火傷や怪我で苦しみうずくまる人々。歩いて市内中心部へと急ぐ。道端にはトタンをかぶせただけの犠牲者の遺体が転がっており足だけがのぞいている。あちこちに馬や犬猫の死骸があり吐き気を催す。

どういうわけか、その日の私たちの服装を今でもよく覚えている。麦わら帽子にランニングシャツ、半ズボンに下駄ばき。水筒とわずかな握り飯を入れたずた袋を肩にかけ、腰ひもには手拭いをぶら下げていた。祖母は紺絣の衣服にモンペ姿。防空頭巾とずた袋をたすき掛けにして履物は地下足袋。

真夏の盛りだったが暑さはほとんど覚えていない。

原爆ドームの左手、瓦礫の空き地は筆者の屋敷跡

コンクリート建ての本川国民学校のそばを通って、やっとの思いで欄干が倒れた相生橋までたどり着く。眼前の産業奨励館の残骸に目を奪われた。屋根の円形ドームと全体の輪郭は間違いなく奨励館だが、ほとんどが無残に崩れ落ちている。川に面して威風堂々、優雅だった産業奨励館はもはや見る影もない。

そして恐る恐る焼け残った燃料倉庫の角を過ぎて、奨励館の左隣りの我が家の跡へ――。

そこには、見る影もなく瓦礫だけがくすぶり続けていた。

高水へ向かった日に、なにげなく見上げた虫籠窓のある土蔵造り。黒格子を巡らした表玄関や見慣れた我が家は何ひとつ残っていなかった。わずかに玄関脇にあったコンクリートの防火用水と手押しポンプが私たちの家の在り処を示す。すべてが焼け落ちて瓦礫の山があるだけである。

焼け残った庭の石灯籠、ひょうたん池の石橋。築山と土蔵の辺りが小高く盛り上がっており、その手前が母屋のあったところだろうか。

祖母の手を握りしめ、泣きながら私は呆然と立ちすくんでいた。

なぜか祖母の目に涙はない。瓦礫をかき分けながら祖母は焼跡へ入っていく。祖母と離れるのが怖い私はついていくしかなかった。足許にはまだ余熱が残っていた。台所の流しのタイルや風呂場の五右衛門釜の残骸がかすかにそれとわかる。

祖母は焼け跡から焼けて柄(え)が失われたスコップを探し出し、台所の付近と両親の居間のあった離れ座敷のあたりを掘り始めた。

瓦や金属片をめくるたびに異様な匂いが鼻につく。

あの時の異様な臭いは今でも忘れられない。後年経験した、鼻を衝(つ)く強烈

広島は一瞬にして焼け野原と化した

な石油コンビナートの化学臭、刺激臭とそれは似ていた。

瓦礫をめくり、あるいは掘り起こしながら、祖母は、父の、母の、弟の名前を呟(つぶや)いていた。

何よりも恐ろしかったのは、あちこちに散乱していた人体の一部と思しき焼け焦げた肉片だった。私はその肉片の幾つかを無意識に手で触れた。となりの産業奨励館で働いていた人々はその瞬間、想像を絶する破壊力と爆風で人体は飛散した。破裂した水道管からあふれる水で何度手を洗っても、その不気味な感触は拭いきれなかった。

ここが爆心地であり、その時まさに人体をむしばむ恐ろしい残留放射能を浴びていたことを知るのは、ずっと後のことであった。

あの時、そこで眼にした情景、耳にした慟哭(どうこく)と悲嘆の声、強烈な異臭、手に触れた不気味なもの——。それらのおぞましい記憶は今も脳裏から離れない。風邪などで高熱が出た時などいつもあの地獄の光景がよみがえる。思い出したくない。口にさえできない。あの地獄の記憶は今も家族にすら話していない。

34

その日、私たちは時が経つのも忘れて我が家の跡を探したが、両親や弟らしき遺体はついに見つからなかった。
　夜、私たちは爆心地から北東に四キロほどのところにある牛田町(うしたまち)の父の友人宅に泊めさせてもらった。焼失こそ免れていたがその家も半壊し主人も酷い火傷を負っていた。その家族も行方不明だという。
　夜、井戸端で体を流し

壊滅した相生橋付近

35　第一章　廣島の終焉

思う存分に冷たい井戸水を飲んだ。

翌八月九日。起きたときから妙に体がだるかった。父たちは避難してきっとどこかで生きている――。一縷の望みを抱いてその日は被災者の収容施設を尋ね歩いた。収容施設といっても、たまたま鉄筋コンクリートか石造りのために崩壊や焼失を免れた建物が、臨時の被災者収容所として使用されているだけであった。

相生橋の東詰めにあった商工会議所を皮切りに、橋を渡って本川国民学校。再び引き返して紙屋町の芸備銀行（現・広島銀行）、住友銀行（現・三井住友銀行）。そして東へ足を延ばして福屋百貨店、南の方角へ、袋町国民学校、市役所、日赤病院にも行ってみた。軍人や救護係と思しき人に家族の行方を尋ねようとしたが、それに応えられる状況ではないことがすぐにわかった。

悪臭の中、全身やけどから激痛を訴え水を求めるおびただしい人々、子どもの泣き叫ぶ声、敷き詰められた筵の上で生死をさまよう被災者の群

れ。いずれも火傷や身体の損傷がひどく手当ての薬品などはない。口から血の泡を吐く断末魔の女学生、そして目を見開いて恨めしそうに虚空を睨む老人もいた。次々に息を引き取る被災者は兵隊が二人がかりで手足を持って運んでいく。死者は山積みされ油を掛けて焼かれる。人間の生命や尊厳、死者への弔いの念はなく、人間性は次第に麻痺していくのだろう。

収容施設で眼にした光景はこの世のものとは思えなかった。なかでも脳裏を離れないのが母親と乳飲み子の姿であった。私の母と弟

市内の随所に被災者収容所

に重なったからかもしれない。すでにこと切れて首が不自然に垂れている母親の乳房を吸い続ける幼な子。あの子は何時まで生き延びただろうか。焼けただれてすでに死んでいる赤ん坊を抱きしめ、子守歌を唄いながらあやす若い母親。私は涙が止まらなかった、なぜこんなことが起きているのか——。

　子ども心に強い無念さと憤怒が沸きあがったことを思い出す。
　生家の近くの川も凄惨であった。春から秋にかけて遊び親しんだ元安川には、おびただしい数の死体が漂流していた。兵隊たちが鳶口（消火道具）を使ってかき寄せては収容船に引き揚げる。子どもらしき遺体には眼球や内臓の破裂など正視できないものも数多くあった。たった数日前には、その川の橋の欄干から飛び込み、対岸まで泳ぎ、魚や貝を採り、ボート遊びに興じていた。それが今では「死の川」と化している。
　途中で生き残った近所の人や知人にも出会ったが、誰も自分の家族を探すのに精いっぱいであった。うつろな目で二言三言、慰めあうだけであった。

ある恐ろしい噂を聞いた。被災の日の午後か翌日らしいが、相生橋の東詰めの角にあった運動具店前——。焼け焦げた電柱に米兵が縛りつけられ死んでいたそうだ。それを目撃した人は少なくない。

米軍機が不時着して捕虜となったアメリカ兵が、広島の憲兵隊司令部で取り調べを受けていた事実はある。しかし、なぜ被爆直後の爆心地へ連行されたのか、その理由はいまだにわからない。いずれにせよアメリカは、自国の兵士をも原爆の犠牲にしたのである。戦争の悲劇や理不尽さがここにもある。

疲れ果てたその夜は我が家へいつも出入りしていた郊外の農家でお世話になった。風呂を使わせてもらい、心づくしの夕飯をごちそうになった。

ようやく祖母と二人、蚊帳（か や）の中でゆっくり休む。昨日や今日の状況では家族はきっと駄目だろう——。

祖母も私もその思いを口にすることはできなかった。

その夜、蚊帳に止まる二匹の蛍を見た。

第一章　廣島の終焉

父は生きていた

　八月十日。朝早く私たちはまた自宅跡へと向かった。横川から寺町筋を通り相生橋から慈仙寺の鼻へ抜けた。対岸の中島本町では、江戸時代からの名刹浄土宗慈仙寺や洋食堂「カフェ・ブラジル」、洋画の映画館「世界館」など、頑丈な建物のすべてが灰燼と化していた。鉄筋コンクリート建ての燃料会館と半壊の藤井倉庫だけをポツンと残して、一面が焼野原であった。

　元安橋を渡って我が家の跡に着くと、見知らぬ屈強な男が三人、庭に残っていた石灯籠を丸太棒と鎖で持ち去ろうとしていた。祖母は恐ろしくて口も効けないでいる。私は思わず「ぼくの家の灯篭をどうするんかっ！」と叫んだ。

　頬骨の出っ張った男が薄ら笑いをしながら私に近づき、突然、私の顔を思い切り殴りつけた。たちまち地面に張り飛ばされ鼻血が出る。彼ら

は悠々と石灯籠と風呂釜を持ち去っていった。

祖母は私を抱き起こし手拭いで血を拭ってくれた。あの時の痛さ悔しさは忘れられない。後で耳にしたことだが、原爆の直後から焼け跡に残った金庫を狙って火事場泥棒が横行したそうだ。家族や家を失い、悲しみに打ちひしがれている者から盗みを働くとは——。人間とはそんなものなのか。

このことはその後、私の原爆への憎しみを増幅させた。

私たちは、情けなく腹立たしい思いをしながら家の跡に立ちすくんでいた。そこへ顔見知りの人が通りがかった。防火用水槽に父の書き置きがあるという。

すぐさま行ってみると、確かに水槽の側面に炭書きの伝言があった。

「八重子へ、高水に行く、連絡せよ。文」

父は生きている！

私たちは、その日の午後、高水へ戻ることにした。

第一章　廣島の終焉

二匹の蛍

母と弟の行方は、とうとうわからなかった。

しかし二人は、すでにこの世の人ではなかった。後でわかったことだが、祖母と私が立っていたすぐ傍の瓦礫の下で、原爆の犠牲になっていたのだ。

「俊彦(私)、お母さんは紘郎(弟)と一緒にここにいるのよ。」

あの時、地面深くから声を出してほしかった。

九日の夜、私たちが見た蚊帳の二匹の蛍……。あれは私たちに別れを告げにきた母と弟だったのかもしれない。

高水へ戻る汽車の中で私は言った。

「お父ちゃんに、あの泥棒たちをやっつけてもらおうよ──。」

祖母がわずかに笑っていた。原爆が落ちてから初めて祖母の笑顔を見た。

高水へ着いたのは夕方だった。すべての音がかき消されたヒロシマと

違って、田んぼでは蛙が鳴き競っていた。

父は自分の無事を陸軍高水病院への軍用電話で知らせており、軍務ですぐに帰れないと伝えていたことも知った。

翌日から高熱が出て私は寝込んでしまった。祖母も体がだるいという。二人とも食欲がなく当時貴重だった卵粥(たまごがゆ)を作ってもらったが、食べたあとすぐに吐き出してしまう。陸軍病院高水分院の院長が往診し、何かの注射をして薬を置いて行ったが吐き気と下痢は収まらなかった。残留放射能による二次被爆のことなど、当時は誰もまだ知らない。

十二日の昼過ぎ、少し体調が回復したので私は外に出てみた。玄関へ通じる石門脇の石塀でぼんやり腰かけていると、神社の森の小道を、杖を頼りにゆっくり近づいてくる軍人らしき人影が見えた。変わり果てた父の姿であった。

走って駆け寄りしがみつくと汗と強い消毒の匂いがした。頭に包帯を巻きつけカーキ色の半そでシャツには血がこびりついていた。腕や手、

43　第一章　廣島の終焉

首筋にも傷だらけでげっそりとやつれていた。

父は言った。

「お母さんと紘郎は、——」

私が大声で泣くのを見て父はうなだれた。

伯父や叔母たち家の者が次々に集まってきて父を取り囲んだ。

「まあよくご無事で。お帰りなさいませ、誰かお水を……。」と手を貸そうとする人もいたが、父はしっかりした足取りで玄関への石畳を進んだ。

そこへ祖父が駆けつけてきた。

父は威儀を正し敬礼をして深々と頭を下げた。

「ただいま戻りました。八重子を死なせたようです。まことに申し訳ありません。」

その時、気丈な祖父の目にも涙が浮かんでいた。

この父の男らしい姿は、その後の私の人生に大きく影響した。あの立派な父のためにも私は何があっても生き延びなければならなかった。

父はあの朝、自宅から五百メートル離れた紙屋町の防空壕で被爆していた。土を盛った壕が崩れ随行の兵が重傷を負ったので、助け出して背負いながら燃えさかる市中を避難したのだという。体中の傷は崩れた土壕から這い出す時に、木切れや釘によってできたものらしい。

父はそれから六日間、指揮官として被災調査や救援などの軍務に懸命であったという。深夜や早朝に自宅

父、出征中の家族。左から祖母、筆者、弟、母

の跡や近くの収容所を訪ね歩き母と弟を探し求めていたそうだ。

私は父に会えたせいか元気を取り戻したような気がした。しかし、父は食べ物が喉を通らず、ひどい下痢症状になり、皮膚に斑点が出て頭髪も抜け始めていた。父は被爆直後から六日間、飲まず食わずで爆心地を歩いていたのだ。体全体に、すさまじいダメージを受けていたのだろう。午後になって、父は歩いて陸軍病院に行くという。皆が止めたが「小父に迷惑をかけたくない。」と言い張り、バケツと手拭いをもって私についてくるように言った。私は父と一緒にいられるのが嬉しくてふたつ返事で従った。

父は遠回りをして炎天下の大歳（おおとし）川沿いの道を歩く、なぜ山影の涼しい道を行かないのか尋ねると父は言った。

「途中で倒れるかもしれないから、倒れたらバケツで川の水をかけてくれ。」

陸軍病院では、父とともに手厚い治療を受けることができた。病院には治療薬や新薬も揃っていた。私が今日まで生き延びることができたの

は、そのおかげかもしれない。

　たしかこの日、祖母一人では父の看病が大変だろうと、身の周りの世話に近所の農家の娘さんが来てくれた。理髪の心得がある娘さんで、洗髪や髭剃りをしてもらう父が、久しぶりに気持ちよさそうな表情だったのを覚えている。

　翌十三日、父は動けなくなった。父はうわ言で母の名を呼んでいた。

　この村にも広島の状況や長崎にも同じ爆弾が落とされたというニュースが伝わってきた。こ

高水中学。右手の校舎を陸軍病院（高水分院）が使用

の戦争には勝てそうもない——、もはや子どもにもわかる状況だった。軍人として生きた父の心中は如何ばかりだっただろう。

八月十五日——父の最期

八月十五日。お盆の中日を迎えたその日は朝から異常に暑くなった。

大人たちは、いずれも沈痛な面持ちで口数も少ない。

祖母に聞くと、正午に重大なラジオ発表があるという。ラジオが故障して聞こえないので父は無理を押して、身の周りの世話をしてもらった娘さんの家へ行った。やがて、家の者に両脇を支えられながら父が帰ってきた。顔に血の気はなく今にも倒れそうだった。

父は離れ座敷に伏せったまま流動食も投薬も断った。そして祖母に言ったという。

「軍人として生きる道はなくなりました。八重子(やえこ)のところへ行きます。俊彦（私）のことをくれぐれも頼みます——。」

父は帝国軍人として敗戦の責任を感じていたのだろうか。陸軍将校として負う罪が家族へ波及することを怖れたのだろうか、今となっては知る由もない。

その日の夕方、父は静かに息を引き取った。

枕元には軍刀が置かれていた。

軍隊経験のある祖父は「わしも田邊の後を追う。」と漏らし、周りをあわてさす一幕もあった。

葬儀は翌々日に行われた。

父は長身だったため普通の寝棺(ねかん)に収まらず、大きい酒樽状の坐棺(ざかん)を使っての葬儀であった。村の寺院の僧侶を呼び簡素な葬式が執り行われた。村の風習に従って大八車(だいはちぐるま)に棺を載せ、笹竹につけた魔除けの白紙をなびかせながら葬式の行列が焼き場まで連なって歩いた。

高水中学の裏山に位置する焼き場で茶毘(だび)に付した。夕闇の中を火炎が渦巻き父は昇天した。三十八歳の生涯である。遠くで夜がらすが鳴いていた。

49　第一章　廣島の終焉

翌日から雨の日が続いた。祖母と二人の離れ座敷には身にしみるような寂しさが立ちこめていた。ふと、夜霧がなびく竹藪(たけやぶ)から青白く、時にうす橙色に光る火の玉がふわりふわりと漂っている。人魂(ひとだま)の不気味さも忘れて「お父ちゃんが、戻ってきたんかね。」とつぶやいた。盆の送り火の夜のことであった。
こうして私は祖母と二人きりになった。何とも言えない不安が込み上げてきた。年寄りと子どもだけでこれからどうやって生きて行けばいいのか――。

第二章 被爆からいかに生きるか

占領されたヒロシマ

父の葬式を終えると田の畔に彼岸花が咲きはじめ、急に秋が近づいてきた。思い出すと、母と弟の葬儀は今もってしていない。「いつか、きっと帰ってくる――。」そう信じていたせいだろうか、はかない思いは六十年以上過ぎても消えていない。

「ヒロシマは、これから七十五年の間、草木は生えないし人間も住むことはできない。」

あまりの惨状に、当時流言がはびこった。それを信じた私たちは広島に帰ることはできなかった。もはや住む家さえない。不憫に思った祖父や伯父は、私と祖母に「いつまで居てもいい。」と言ってくれた。

しかし祖母にしてみれば、息子と嫁が亡くなってなお、いつまでも嫁の実家にいるわけにはいかない。やがて居場所がなくなることを祖母は知っていたのだろう。

私は二学期から高水の国民学校へ通うことになった。
　学校は大半が農家の子だった。私は「非農家」と呼ばれ、ことあるごとに苛められた。「負けるものか。」と虚勢を張っても多勢に無勢、いつもこづかれ叩かれて泣かされていた。
　「いじめ」はいつの時代にもあるものらしい。祖母に助けを求めても「それでも、お父さんの子どもなの。」とたしなめられるばかりで頼るすべもない。
　やがて、米軍のマッカーサー元帥ら進駐軍が日本に上陸した。大人は落ち着かない様子であった、とくに軍隊帰りは恐れおののいていた。私は、何とか父の敵を討てないものかと思案していた。座敷の刀掛けに父の遺品の軍刀が収まっている。抜いてみると、ずしりと重く立派な業物である。そのさまを祖母に見つかった。
　「これで父の敵を討ちたい。」というと祖母は笑いながらも涙ぐんでいた。祖母も同じ思いだったに違いない。
　すすき、ききょう、女郎花、秋の七草が咲き季節が深まる頃、高水の

田舎にも進駐軍がやってきて、刀剣や銃砲など残留武器を接収しにかかった。「隠匿すると重く罰せられる」と村の駐在から脅され、やむなく祖父は父の軍刀を供出した。

高水の駐在巡査とアメリカ兵がジープでやってきた。彼らを睨みつけたが子どもの私は見向きもされなかった。兵士らは群がる子どもたちにチョコレートやチューインガムを与えていた。私は必死にやせ我慢をして受け取らなかった。

廣島時代と違って田舎の学校では、学校農園での農作業や畑仕事がほとんどだった。勉強らしい勉強はなく、たまにあちこちが黒く塗りつぶされた教科書を読み、粗末なわら半紙をノート代わりに使って書きとりや算数をした。みじめな敗戦後の混乱の中で、中身のほとんどない学校生活を送らざるを得なかった。

やがて年が明けた。田舎暮らしには慣れてきたが母がいない母の実家では居づらかった。とくに祖母には居場所がなかったことだろう。私たちは疎開先をあとにして別の親戚や知人を頼って、あちこちで不

安定な生活を送るようになった。私の家は広島県北の農村にかなりの田畑や山林を所有していたが、農地改革により「不在地主」とされて国に無償で取り上げられた。祖母は悔し涙で途方に暮れていた。

まったく収入のない年寄りと子どもが暮らしを維持するためには、疎開させていた貴重な家財道具や衣装、骨董品などを売るほかなかった。それ

進駐軍のヒロシマ入り

が尽きると残ったのは市内の土地だけだった。それさえも「ヒロシマには人間は住めない」という風聞を盾に、悪質な大人やブローカーがタダ同然で買いとっていった。当時、そんな光景は日常茶飯事だった。

普段の暮らしでも、年寄りと子どもだけの所帯は徹底して蔑視され、差別され、そして苛められた。いつも脅え不安を抱え、たらいまわしにあいながら各地を転々として二年が過ぎた。

その間、時々広島にも戻った。人が住めないはずの土地にバラックが建ち人々が徐々に暮らし始めている。地面には緑が芽吹き、野鳥や虫の姿も見られる。

「人が住めるのではないか——。」

私たちは狐につままれたような感覚に襲われた。

やがて、原爆ドームに隣接する私たちの屋敷跡は、「都市復興建設法」により接収されることになった。その代替地として市街地西の外れの山麓にわずかな土地をあてがわれた。祖母は「もっとましな場所を」と掛けあったそうだが、非力な年寄りとして相手にされなかった。「土地台帳

が焼失して不明」を理由に、非情にも面積は四分の一に削減された。
働き盛りの大人が世帯主の場合、逆に二倍三倍に拡大された例もあっ
たそうだ。年寄りと子どもだけの世帯であったから無情にも不当な扱い
を受けたのだ。

何時も「父さえ生きていたら――。」そう嘆かずにはいられなかった。
祖母と私は意を決し、その換地(かんち)を手放して広島市内の中心部に小さい
家を建てることにした。誰にも気兼ねのない二人だけの、ささやかな安
住の地がやっと見つかった。

戦後「ヒロシマ」の真実

その年の秋、私は広島大学付属小学校に復学の申請をした。しかし受
付の事務員は学籍名簿の私の欄を見て、ただ一言いっただけだった。
「今さら復学は無理です。」指差された名簿の私の名前の欄には「原爆
死」と記されてあった。当時の私は、いつもの苛(いじ)めや差別に慣れて麻痺

してしまっていた。「またか」と諦めて仕方なく市立の小学校に編入した。
この頃は、両親がいないことで止めどない寂しさを感じることが多かった。父兄参観、運動会、学芸会、学習発表……。祖母は病気がちでほとんど来ることができなかった。いつも独りぼっちで我慢した。
どうしても耐えられなくなると、両親が眠る菩提寺の墓地を訪れた。原爆ドームの側にある西向寺の被爆で欠けた冷たい墓石の前で泣いていると、父母の声が聞こえた気がする。「泣きたいだけ泣くがいい、気が済んだら強く生きるのだ、いつもそばで見守っているから。」
そのまま夜が更けることもあった。たくさんの霊が眠るその墓地を怖いと思ったことは、一度もない。
この西向寺には、本尊の阿弥陀如来像、両脇に親鸞聖人と蓮如上人の絹絵図があった。これらは原爆直前に疎開して奇蹟的に焼失を免れていた。祖母はお参りするたびに私に語り諭したものだ。
「お上人の絵巻きは、明治時代に本堂修築の記念として田邉家の祖先が寄進したものなの。原爆で何もかも焼けたが、この仏画をご先祖様と

思って家を再興しなくてはならない。間違っても人様から後ろ指を指されるようなことをしないように。」

それ以来、私はこの歳になるまで墓参やお寺参りを欠かしたことはない。迷い事や困難に遭うと必ず訪れて祖先や人智を超えた存在に問いかけ、ひたすらすがった。仏教への信仰は、それ自体が自分自身との対峙（たいじ）でもあったような気がする。祖母から教わった念仏を唱えていると不思議に心が安らぎ、難事や災事解決への糸口が見つかった。

清浄な信仰の心とは裏腹に人間の世界には醜くいこと、汚いことが多く存在する。被爆直後のヒロシマと、その後の人心の荒廃がまさにそうだった。

「原爆」という、あまりにも悲惨でむごたらしい被害。世間の目はヒロシマへの同情や憐憫（れんびん）があり、すべてが浄化美化され、その陰で行われた悪徳や不正行為は隠蔽（いんぺい）されてしまった。戦争による混乱や未曾有の災害に乗じた心ない人間による非道で許されざる行為、人間の性善説を否定せざるを得ない事態が起きることもまた、私たちは知らなくてはならな

いまだに被爆生存者の多くが疑惑を拭い去れないのが、被爆後に始まった搾取と不正と悪徳の記憶である。あの頃のヒロシマは犯罪の温床だった。焼け出されて着のみ着のままの被爆者から、なけなしの品をだまし取ったり、ただ同然で買いあさった者もいた。戦時中の軍や民間の隠匿物資を探し出し、物不足の闇市で売りさばいて不当に暴利を貪った連中もいた。

さらに、原爆による一家全滅や子どもだけが残った所帯の預貯金はどこへ消えたのだろうか。受け取り手のない資産はどうなったのか。戦時中の国策として預貯金を奨励、おびただしい額が眠っていたはずだ。銀行をはじめ郵便局や証券会社、それらの金融機関が我がものにしたのか。数多くの犠牲者の尊い生命を代償に、彼らは莫大な不当利益を得たのか。頑丈な地下金庫は原爆からの焼失を免れているという。どんなに時が過ぎても、この「不都合な真実」ともいうべき隠蔽疑惑を払拭することはできない。

空前の破壊の後、被災地では復興が始まった。地元や周辺の土建業者はこぞって再建に取り組んだ。材料不足や大工左官の人手不足を理由に、容赦なく価格を吊り上げ、あるいは不当な代金を請求した事例も多かった。その後、ゼネコンに成り上がった業者も少なくない。

原爆直後の駅前や盛り場の闇市周辺では目を覆う暴力沙汰が絶えなかった。警棒以外に武器を持たない警官や交番巡査は成す術（すべ）もなく見て見ぬふりをし、凶悪犯罪への役にはまったくたたず町の治安は極端に地に落ちていた。

とくに敗戦により解放された外国人の凶悪犯罪や横暴は目に余った。そして、それらを鎮めたのは任侠の気風が残る土地のやくざや極道らである。

その後、彼らは金目当ての暴力団に変貌して、市民を巻き込む組同士の抗争や悪質な犯罪を繰り返し、社会の敵として世間のひんしゅくを買うことになるが、あの時、町の治安を曲がりなりにも維持したのは義侠心のあるやくざや極道たちである。

当時、人々は彼らを「暴力団」とは呼ばなかった。凶悪で卑劣な輩から災難に遭うか弱い女性や年寄りを救い、力をもって解決するところをこの目でたびたび見た。彼らの姿は、講談や浪曲でおなじみの「清水次郎長」「吉良の仁吉」「国定忠治」を彷彿とさせた。今となってはその面影すらない。

先にも述べたつらい思い出であるが、祖母が折に触れ思い余って呟いたことがある。

「……俊ちゃん、みんなが待つあの世へ行こうか。」

それが何を意味するのかはわかっていた、思わず首を強く横に振ったものだ。当時悲嘆に暮れて自ら「死」を選んだり、原爆後遺症で一家が絶えるなど、ごくありふれたことだった。そんなことになるものか、あってたまるか。遠い祖先からの家系を絶やしてなるものか。きっと生き延びて、生き延びて、かならず家を再興させてやる。あの時、私の心に強烈な自立への決心が芽生え「生への意識」が、ふつふつと湧き上がったのである。

運命との出会い

十四歳の時だった。それからの人生に大きく影響する運命的な出会いがあった。

中学二年の春、私の学校に国語の女性教師が赴任してきた。彼女は師範学校を卒業したばかりでまだ若く清楚で美しかった。生徒ばかりでなく同僚の教師からも憧れの的だったと思う。そのY先生から習った「徒然草」の一節は今でも忘れていない。私の家は学校の近くだったこともあり放課後によく校庭の石碑辺りで先生と語り合った。

今にして思えば、当時の私は彼女に亡き母のやさしい面影を重ねていたのかもしれない。原爆のことをあまり話さないのも嬉しかった。後でわかったことだが彼女も被爆者であった。

いきおい国語の勉強には力が入った。その後、文科系に進んだのもこの先生の影響が大きかったのかもしれない。あれから五十年以上が過ぎ

ているが、今でもことあるごとに電話や手紙を頂き、ずっと私の仕事を温かく見守ってもらっている。心づくしの立派な外国製万年筆も頂いた、これは私のちょっとした自慢である。

そんなある日のことだった。国語の時間に作文の宿題が出され当時では珍しい上質の原稿用紙を用意して、原爆を体験した生徒は次週までに手記を書いてくるように、といわれた。

忌まわしい原爆のことなど書きたくもなかった。しかし憧れの先生の指示とあっては書かないわけにもいかない。

被爆から五年が経っていた。自分の中で原爆への怒りや憎しみは以前よりは少し整理がつきつつもあった。社会科の教科書で知った。原子力は兵器として開発されたが、核エネルギーを応用して人類の平和や幸福のためにも利用できるのだと。原爆への憎しみを封印するために、そんなふうに無理やりに自分に思い込ましたのかもしれない。

その時に提出した私の手記はやがて本になることになった。Y先生もとても喜んでくれた。

手記が載った『原爆の子――広島の少年少女のうったえ』

その本は、広島大学の長田新教授（当時）の編纂による原爆体験手記集であった。

『原爆の子～広島の少年少女のうったえ～』として出版された。

大学の教室で出版記念会が開かれ百五人の執筆者は全員、長田教授から一人ひとりに本が手渡された。表紙をめくると「幼き神の子の声を聞け」と記され、長田教授の署名が添えられていた。

この『原爆の子』は出版されるやいなや評判を呼んだ。

長田教授の呼びかけにより、小学生から大学生まで手記の執筆者を中心として「原爆の子友の会」が結成された。会長に高校生のNさん、副会長に女子高生のMさんと私が選ばれた。

「友の会」は長田教授とその子息らの世話と指導により、子どもの立場から被爆体験の証言をはじめ、原爆をテーマにした演劇の上演やコーラスなどの催し、平和関連団体との連携交流など、かなり積極的に活動を行った。いわば子どもを中心にした平和運動、反原爆活動でもあった。

頻繁に行われる会合では、私と同じく原爆により親兄弟を亡くした仲

66

長田教授と語らう筆者（右端）

『原爆の子』寄稿者たち

間がたくさんいた。同じ体験を有する彼らの優しさや温かさにも心がなごんだ。祖母と二人暮らしの寂しさからも解放される時間だった。

やがて『原爆の子』を原作として、新藤兼人監督による劇映画が製作されることになった。

新藤監督をはじめとするロケハン（撮影の下見）スタッフを迎えたのは「友の会」のメンバーであった。私たちは子どもの視点で被爆前後の暮らしを具体的に説明したり、市内の原爆の爪痕をくわしく案内した。映画の一シーンに我が家の跡で撮影された場面があるが、そのあらわれである。

私は、中学三年生の夏休みをほとんどこの活動に費やしていた。今思えば「友の会」の活動に熱中したのは、独りぼっちの寂しさを忘れることができたからだ。共通の体験をした仲間たちと知り合い心が通いあうのが嬉しかったのだ。

「友の会」の運動にのめりこむほどに学校の成績は下がり、親しい学友も次第に離れていった。学校では校長や主任に呼び出され「友の会」の

活動を控えるよう再三注意されるようになった。

そうこうするうちに映画製作への支援体制や物語の展開をめぐって、新藤監督と長田教授の間でトラブルが起こった。ついには「友の会」として新藤作品をボイコットすることが決められてしまった。

そして、新たな別の映画の製作が始まった。日教組が支持する関川秀雄監督の作品であり、「友の会」はこちらの作品への協力活動を開始した。結局、大人たちのこの間のいきさつは今もって不可解で不明瞭である。新藤作品の不純で醜い政治抗争に巻き込まれたとしか言いようがない、なんとも不快な出来事であった。

純粋な「平和希求」が目的のはずの活動なのに……。子ども心にも強い不信感と違和感を覚えた。いきおい私は長田家のやり方や「友の会」の活動にも疑問を持ち嫌気がさすようになった。さらに「友の会」の中には、手記の執筆者ではない者や原爆体験と無関係な者が加わるようになって、仲間意識や和やかな絆も次第に薄れていってしまった。自分自身の中でも、友の会活動に対して引き時への決断を迫られるこ

とになった。

　私は祖母と相談して広島を離れることにした。原爆は幼い頃の私の大切な家族や生活のすべてを奪い取った。少年期になって、また原爆に再び窮地に追いこまれていくような気がした。原爆はまたしても私を苛め通すのか──。どんなことがあっても、もうこれ以上原爆には関わりたくない。被爆体験と訣別し原爆に絶縁状をたたきつけよう。

　こうして私は「原爆の子友の会」を辞めた。強い決意のもとに長田教授から頂いた『原爆の子』の初版本をごみ箱に捨てた。

　そして、かつての疎開先の高水に行き、伯父が校長をしている高校へ入学した。老いた祖母を残していくのは気が引けたが、ほかならぬ祖母が強く背中を押してくれた。こうして私は父祖の地、原爆の地ヒロシマから遠ざかった。

　しかし、皮肉なことに、この『原爆の子』での体験こそがその後の私の運命を決定づけることになった。

　新藤監督の「原爆の子」、関川監督の「ひろしま」。私がこの二作品の

製作に関わることができたのは、今思えば大変な運命的なことであり、実体験を通じて映画づくりの魅力を肌で感じ取っていたのだ。ちなみに両作品の評価をするならば、迷わず新藤作品に分配が上がる。
「自分の将来はこれしかない。そうだ映画監督になろう——。」
私はあの時、そう心に決めたのだった。

映像ジャーナリストの世界へ

高水での高校生活は、ヒロシマでのぬぐえぬ不信感や不安定な心もしだいに安らぎ充実したものだった。
母が生まれ育った地、父が最期を迎えた処、

安穏を求めた高水高校時代の筆者

71　第二章　被爆からいかに生きるか

純朴さが残る風土は孤独な私を優しく包んでくれる。小学校時代に私を苛（いじ）めた連中も今度は温かく迎えてくれた。

原爆とは何の関わりもない日常の中で映画作家への夢だけは大切に温存していた。そして、次第にその夢は強固なものになっていった。私はもはや周囲に煩（わずら）わされることなく、歩むべき道をめざしてゆっくりと人生設計を立てることができた。

当時、映画監督を目指すには、監督の弟子入りをして助手から修業を重ね、いわゆる「たたきあげ」の経験を積んで独立するか、あるいは専門の大学で研修を積むかのどちらかであった。私は後者を選んだ。

国内では唯一、日本大学の芸術学部に映画学科があり、その中に「監督養成コース」がある。かなりの難関であるがこれしかない。当時、日大の芸術学部に入るのに必要な受験科目は、国語、社会、英語。強い意志のもとに理数系科目については低空飛行を決めこみ、受験に必要な三科目に集中して三年間の勉学に励んだ。

時たま見るアメリカ映画の名作や西部劇映画の影響か、英語の勉強に

は興味を持った。ラジオで岩国の米軍極東放送（FEN）を聞き、生の英語を学んだ。聞き慣れてくるとやがてニュース番組から世界の動き、さらに外国の興味ある情報がわかるようになる。田舎にいても国際情勢やアメリカの生活文化に触れ親しむことができた。

FENの音楽番組ではジャズやポピュラー、ラテン音楽に心をひかれた。戦後の歌謡曲全盛時代にあって、日本の音楽とはリズムもメロディーもまるで違う、すべてが軽快で本当に心地よく聞こえてくる。トミー・ドーシー、グレン・ミラー、ベニー・グッドマンの軽快なスウィングジャズ。ドリス・デイ、ビング・クロスビー、ナット・キング・コールの心に沁みるポピュラーソング。ザビア・クガー、ペレス・プラード、ロス・パンチョスの情熱的なラテンリズム……。

むろんテレビもまだなく娯楽の少ない時代、いずれも心を躍らせながら聴きいった。

戦時中を通じて軍歌や童謡しか知らない私にはすべてが新鮮だった。

「こんな素晴らしい音楽を生み出した国と戦争をしたのか。」と暗澹たる

思いがしたものだ。

高水高校で私が初めて見つけたささやかな幸せと日常、その生活を支えたのは父の軍人恩給と遺族年金、祖母からの仕送りであった。その祖母も原爆後遺症でこの世を去った。高校二年の秋である。こうして私は家族のすべてを失い、この世でただ一人の身となった。

被爆直後から祖母は私の親代わりだった。わずかな収入をやりくりしながら生活を支える祖母、そんな祖母に無理を承知でわがままを言って困らせたこともあった。

高校の時も一人広島に残り、生活を切り詰めて送金を続けた祖母の苦労はいかばかりであったことだろう。祖母への不孝はどんなに悔やんでも悔やみきれない。原爆で頼る家族を失い「孫の育成のみの日々」で老後を送り、人生を薄幸のままあの世へ旅立たせてしまった。

今も毎日仏壇に手を合わせ、取り返しのつかない不孝への詫びとともに、せめてもの供養を続けている。

やがて私は努力の甲斐あって日本大学芸術学部の映画学科に入学でき

た。当時では唯一の映画界への輝かしい登竜門であった。

大学への進学にはかなりの費用を必要とした。当時の制度では二十歳の成人を迎えるとともにすべての恩給や年金が打ち切られる。我が家には預貯金などあろうはずがなく、自力で暮らしを立て学資は自分で賄う以外にない。

叔父の力添えで東京奥多摩の小河内ダム建設現場で働いた。週の前半は練馬区江古田の大学に行き、後半は奥多摩の工事現場で働きながら過ごした。

当然、遊ぶ金も時間もなく、ただひたすら勉学に励んだ。教養課程では映画修業の基本に関わる映画芸術論や

苦学時代の筆者、ダムの建設現場で

75　第二章　被爆からいかに生きるか

製作論、映画史をはじめ、文学論、心理学、社会学、東西の歴史学、そして哲学……。

これらの学問を真剣に学んだことは後の映像作家人生に大きく役立った。専門課程の中ほどで世の中の出来事や社会問題を、独自の視点で描く「記録映画」を歩むべき道として決めた。

ドキュメンタリー作品の監督として、あるいは脚本家として、あるいは製作者として、私は「記録映画」をライフワークとして選んだのである。

大学の二年生の時だった。風邪をこじらせ高熱で寝込んだがなかなか回復しなかった。埼玉県所沢の病院に入院して検査を受けたところ、白血球が異常をきたしていることがわかった。医師はカルテを見て広島出身だとわかると被爆の影響による呼吸器障害の疑いがあると診断した。ショックだった。日頃から原爆のことは極力忘れるようにしていただけに。

その後、就職や結婚、子どもの出産……と、そのたびに私は原爆の影に脅え恐れ慄（おのの）くことになった。

映像作家への道

　一九七三年（昭和四十八年）。「自立への挑戦」私は一年をかけて、単独で記録映画の修業を目的に海外での撮影に旅立つことにした。大学卒業後、地元の中国新聞社の映像部門へ就職したが、十三年間勤めた新聞社に見切りをつけた。この決意は幼い子どもを含む家族を抱えた身で無謀な挑戦であることは百も承知であった。

　新聞社では急速なテレビ化の影響で私の望んだ映像部門も映画からテレビへとシフトしていた、私はテレビの仕事はやりたくなかった。じっくりと作り上げる映画と違って、それはただ消費されるだけの一過性のメディア媒体であるからだ。

　十五歳、中学三年生のあの時から私はひたすら映画監督になりたかった。初心を貫いて難関の映画の道に進んだ。私は映画の職人として生涯

第二章　被爆からいかに生きるか

を全うしたかった。

新たな人生を自力で切り開かなくてはならない。時間をかけ、それからの人生設計を思案する目的も兼ねて赤道を越えた未開の地への旅立ちを思い付いたのだった。

私の念頭には大学時代に観た、あるアメリカ映画のことがあった。南海の楽園を描いたジョシュア・ローガン監督のミュージカル映画「南太平洋」である。あまりの映像美に私は感動し、強く憧れ、心酔していた。この地球上にあのような美しい海や島が本当にあるのだろうか。文明からほど遠い地で人間と自然はどのような暮らしをしているのだろうか。では人々はどのように共生しているのだろうか。

「地上最後の楽園」といわれた南太平洋とはいったいどんなところなのか。かのポール・ゴーギャンが芸術の都パリを捨ててまで住み着いたタヒチとは、サマセット・モームが名作の短編「雨」を書き上げたアメリカンサモアのパゴパゴとは。

物質世界から取り残された非日常の世界を自分の目で確かめカメラに

収めよう——。折しも日本は、ようやく戦後の混乱が落ち着き高度経済成長期に入っていた。そして、そのひずみとして「公害問題」が立ちはだかった時代でもあった。

それまで海外に行ったことなどなかったが、現地の情報に詳しい太平洋文化研究所（呉市出身の岩佐嘉親所長）の協力を得て、私は周到に準備に取りかかった。

対象は、赤道から南半球へかけてのミクロネシア、メラネシア、ポリネシア、広大な南太平洋のほぼ全域である。現在と違っ

映画撮影機と修業中の筆者

第二章　被爆からいかに生きるか

てそれらはすべて「知られざる世界」であった。公害の片鱗（へんりん）すら見当たらない自然美のニューヘブリデスをはじめ、フィジー、サモア、トンガ、そしてタヒチの国々や島々。そこでは経済的な豊かさはなくとも満ち足りた自然環境の中で人々は心豊かな暮らしを営んでいるという。押し寄せる文明の波に翻弄されながらも民俗的風習を大切に守り続けている。まる一年をかけた「南太平洋の旅」は予想をはるかに上回る価値のあるものとなった。

香港から中型のプロペラ機に乗ってパプアニューギニアのポートモレスビーへ、赤道に近づくにしたがって眼下の景色は原色に輝く。コバルトブルーの海、エメラルド色のサンゴ礁、純白のビーチ、緑を敷き詰めたようなココナッツ椰子のプランテーション、そこには高層ビルも高速道路もない、コンクリートの欠片（かけら）さえない。いつまでも飽くことなく機中から私はただただ、あまりの美しさに呑み込まれていた。

ポートモレスビーからソロモン群島のホニアラへ、小型機でメラネシアの島々を乗り継ぎながらニューヘブリデスのエスピリッツ・サント島

へたどり着いた。快晴の南太平洋の小島は心地よい潮風とともに息を呑む美しさ、トロピカルフラワーがそこかしこに咲き乱れている。サンゴ礁の入り江ではアウトリガー（転倒防止翼）付のカヌーが浮かび、住民たちの原始的な漁が目を奪う。

そして、ここを起点として、ゆっくりと南太平洋の取材旅行をスタートさせた。ニューヘブリデス群島から魅惑のタヒチへ、私は時間を忘れて旅をした。そして手つかずの自然やそこに生きる人々の生活風習を記録映画と写真に収め続けた。

アウトリガー（転倒防止翼）付のカヌー

不思議とその間に考えることはこんなことだった。平和とは何だろう、戦争はなぜ起きるのだろう──。

私が訪れたずっと後に独立して、バヌアツ共和国となったニューヘブリデスのマレクラ島、その海辺の集落では住民総出の漁を目にした。夜の満潮時に棕櫚の皮で編んだ網を入り江に沈めておく、翌朝の干潮時に網を絞って海面をたたき魚を追い込みながら捕まえる。獲れた魚は村人で均等に分け合っていた。

島々の集落から集落へは波の静かなサンゴ礁をアウトリガーのカヌーで行き来する。郵便配達や物資の輸送運搬もすべてカヌーで行われていた。

素朴な土器づくりの光景も目にした。赤土の粘土をこねて適度な丸みをつけるために女性の膝頭で整形をする、立て膝での作業は、にぎやかなおしゃべりの中で進められていた。

形になった土器は盛り土式の窯で一晩をかけて竹で焼きあげる。温度が低いのでいささか脆いが立派に使える素朴な暮らしの土鍋が出来あが

る。
　働き盛りの男たちは椰子の木陰で「ティキ」と呼ばれる南太平洋独得の木彫りの神像づくりを手掛けていた。その作業は念入りで急がない。時間はいくらでもあるからだ。
　「民俗的な視点から、暮らしを背景に人間を描く──。」
　私は後半生の映像製作の手法や理念を、この旅で習得し確立したように思う。

第三章 運命を生きる
――廣島復元事業への決意

海外で知った私の中の「ヒロシマ」

この、ほぼ一年をかけた旅行の成果は、帰国後に東京新宿の紀伊國屋ギャラリー、広島天満屋ギャラリー、広島銀行本店ロビーなどで「南太平洋の旅」と題する写真展で発表した。記録映画フィルムは地元の民放テレビ開局記念映像として繰り返し放映された。

今にして思えば、あの大切な時間をかけた旅は、私が失った「廣島」の原型を心情的に外部に求める旅でもあった。

原爆の投下により私は家族をはじめ何もかも失った。そして広島はそれまでの歴史や伝統文化さえも失ってしまった。今の広島はあの頃の廣島とは繋がっていない。原爆によって何もかも切断させられてしまったのだ。

人々のふるさとへの心情、郷土への誇りや愛着、風習や民俗、長い時によって培われた歴史文化、それらすべてが織り込まれた廣島という

「場」をも、原爆は完膚なきまでに破壊し消失させてしまったのだ。
私はその「場」を取り戻したかった、それは私という存在と不可分のものであるからだ。形は違えど南太平洋にはそれがまだ残っていた。私は無意識にそれを紡ぎ織っていたのだと思う。
そしてこの旅は、私が本来の自分に立ち還るためのもうひとつの手段であり、手助けをしてくれたように思う。
当時の南太平洋は、まだ観光開発が進んでいなかった。いきおい旅程の大半は原住民の集落で寝起きをすることになる。
活火山で知られるニューヘブリデス諸島のタナ島を訪れた時のことだった。数週間にわたって海岸の粗末なバンガローに滞在し、同じように取材に訪れていたアメリカ人ジャーナリストに出会った。記録写真の撮影や紀行文の執筆などの仕事の合間に彼とよく語りあった。
赤道直下の満天星空のもと、ワインや雨水で割ったウイスキーを傾けながら、お互いの仕事のことを語り明かしたものだ。そうするうちに、あまり話したくない触れられたくない話題ではあったがヒロシマの話に

87　第三章　運命を生きる──廣島復元事業への決意

彼は言った。原爆について「核爆発を利用しているが通常爆弾の大規模なものと認識している」と。原爆はあくまで「戦争の早期終結を目的としたもので廣島の軍事施設が目標」と。そして彼の口から出たのは原爆の規模と死傷者数、軍事施設の壊滅状況などの数値データ、ただそれだけであった。

彼は普通のアメリカ人ではない、世界的な有力紙にも寄稿する見識あるジャーナリストである。その彼にして原爆をその程度に理解しているのか、私は驚き思わず反論せずにはいられなかった。

原爆は何の前触れや予告もなく、ある日、普通の市民生活の上に投下されたのだと。犠牲者の大半は普通の市民であり、彼らは何が起きたのか、何もわからないまま、避難するいとまもなく、ほぼ瞬間に生命を奪われたのだ。中でも爆心地においては何の罪もない幼な子や年寄り、それに婦女子たちが大勢地獄の惨状に巻き込まれた事実を。

核爆発とともに五千度を上回る熱波が地上を襲い、想像を絶する衝撃波と放射線が、町や家、住む人間、そのすべてを焼き尽くした。鉄を溶かす溶鉱炉でさえ温度は千五百度、陶芸の窯の焼成温度が千度内外である。原子爆弾の炸裂、それがいかにすさまじい灼熱であったことか。そして地域の歴史や伝統文化をふくめ、町の営みや生活環境のすべてが全滅したのだ。中でも放射線障害はいまだに人体を蝕み、後遺症として多くの被爆者を苦しめ続けているのだと。

彼は長い沈黙の後でただ一言だけを呟いた。「そんなこととは、まったく知らなかった。」

このことが、後に私が「爆心地復元事業」をライフワークとして取り組む遠因ともなった。

私は南太平洋から戻ると、再び念願の映像づくり一筋の道に舞い戻った。

一九七五年（昭和五十年）、私は「株式会社ナック映像センター」を設立した。広島地方における記録映画製作会社の第一号である。

89　第三章　運命を生きる——廣島復元事業への決意

社名の「ナック（KNACK）」はあまり一般的な用語ではないが、れっきとした英単語で「熟練の技、卓越した技術、優れた仕事」を意味する。私が取り組みたいと願う仕事のスタイルを如実に言い表している言語なのだ。海外滞在中に意味のあるこの名称を使うことを決めていた。

そして新聞社の新入社員時代、苦労して映画製作技術のすべてを体得したことが、この会社設立時の大きなバックボーンになった。あの時の労苦と体験がなければ私は会社を興すことはできなかった。

当時は、まだビデオ映像は一般化しておらず、テレビにおいても実況の生放送以外は映画フィルム中心の時代である。最初は小規模経営だから事業計画から経営実務、それに労務や経理まですべてをこなさなければならない。十年間は寝る間も惜しんで働く日々だった。経営的に苦しい時期には、かつて働いていた新聞社からCM制作の仕事など温かい支援も頂いた。

広報映画、観光映画、教育映画、医学映画など、地元の企業や大学、さらに官公庁からの業務受注はだんだんと増えていった。地域振興を啓

産業奨励館破壊の瞬間（CG画像）

発する作品や医学の新技術を紹介する記録映画、学校や企業の教育プログラム、海外でのロケ……。

結局、不本意ながらテレビの映像もたくさん制作したが、ただ消費されるだけの安易な番組は作らなかった。これは私のささやかな矜持でもある。南太平洋で身をもって会得した「暮らしと民俗」をベースに地域を描くテレビ番組を数多く作成した。

郷土再発見シリーズと題して「瀬戸内、民芸の旅」にはじまり、「山陰山陽、川の旅」「港の旅」「ふるさと出会いふれあい」「いい旅味な旅」「文学の旅つれづれ紀行」「ふるさと歴史人物紀行」「ふるさとの匠と技〜中国地方の伝統工芸をたずねて〜」といった毎週放送の番組、五百本を上回る郷土シリーズは中国五県のネットワークで十年以上にわたって放映され、微力ながら地域文化の振興や向上に貢献することができた。

私は映像の道を着実に歩み続け、広島の地で多くの仕事を手掛けていたが、一貫して「原爆」というテーマは回避してきた。いぶかりながら理由を聞かれたときには、ただ「したくないからだ」とだけ答えていた。

しかしながら心の奥底では、原爆を拒み続けたことへの「後ろめたさ」があった。そして私は何か後世に残るような仕事をしたいと切望するようになっていた。

ピースサインの女子高生

そんな時のことだった。

一九九七年（平成九年）、私は還暦を迎えた。

秋の彼岸だったと思うが、墓参を終えて原爆ドームの横

会社設立後、錦帯橋ロケ

第三章　運命を生きる──廣島復元事業への決意

を通りかかった。

この一昨年、原爆ドームは「世界遺産」に登録されていた。国はもとより海外からも注目され、あらゆるメディアが取り上げて観光客は例年以上に急増していた。

修学旅行らしき女子高生の一団が記念撮影をしていた。その一人から「すみません」と声をかけられカメラのシャッターを押してほしいという。

引き受けてカメラのファインダーを覗き込むと、今も母と弟が地面深くに眠っている我が家の跡がフレームの片隅に見えた。次の瞬間、女子高生たちは満面の笑みを浮かべて「イエーィ」の声とともにVサインをしてみせた。

私はハッとした。

ここでいったい何が起きたのか、彼女たちはわかっているのだろうか。

もし知っているならば到底できる所作ではない。

厳島神社でも錦帯橋でも、きっと彼女らは同じように笑顔でピースサ

インをしながら記念写真に納まっていることだろう、彼女たちにとって原爆ドームは、宮島や錦帯橋と同じ観光名所のひとつに過ぎないのだろうか──。

あの日、ここで起きたことはすでに忘却されているのだ。女子高生らはきちんと礼をいい、その後も明るく和やかにふるまっていた。その屈託のない表情を見ていると、彼女たちを責める気にはとてもなれなかった。

衣食住や娯楽にも恵まれ、生命の危険にさらされることもなく、平和な時代に生きている若い世代たちをうらやましく思った。そしてできることなら、彼らがこれからの人生を今と同じようにあってほしいと願ったものだ。

これが私の終盤の生き方を決める決定的なきっかけとなった。最早これ以上自分を偽って生きることはできない。もう後戻りはできない。私はずっと「原爆」に背を向けて生きてきた。これからは「原爆」と真正面に向き合いすべてをかけて取り組んでみよう。これこそが自分に

第三章　運命を生きる──廣島復元事業への決意

しかできない歴史の空白を埋める仕事だ──。かたく決意をした。この日を起点として私の後半生のライフワークが始まった。史上初の「爆心地復元事業」への取り組みである。

在りし日の「ふるさと」を探す

被爆以前の産業奨励館については、当時正確な情報はほとんど見当たらなかった。中でも不明とされていたのが内部の各階の施設や構造、各部屋の様子や細部の状況、とくに色彩だった。わずかに残る写真もすべてモノクロである。外壁や窓枠、カーテン、天井、照明、塔屋（とうおく）のステンドグラス、屋根、ドーム部分はいったい何色だったのか。

私は、それまで封印していた遠い記憶を呼び覚ました。

世間が知りたがったのは次の点である。産業奨励館はどんな建物だったのか、どんな構造の建築様式で、産業の何を奨励し、内部の展示空間や配置はどのようになっていたのか。各階にはどんな部屋があり、どん

な人たちが何をしていたのか。

そして、あの日、奨励館では何人が働いていたのか。産業奨励館の東隣りで、我が家同然に朝から晩まで過ごしていた私にとってはいずれも何でもないことだった。色見本があればどの箇所の色でも的確に指差すことができるだろう。

──やってみよう。我が映像人生の終幕を飾るにふさわしい仕事だ。私は原爆ドームの在りし日の姿、被爆以前の産業奨励館時代の全貌とそれを取り巻く伝統的な町並みをよみがえらせる画期的なプロジェクトをたち上げた。

最初に重要なのは産業奨励館の再現である。どのような方法があるのか模索を続けた。

ミニチュアセット方式を専門業者に打診すると、リアルな当時の町並みを含めて数千万円もかかりとても手が届かない。アニメーションも稚拙な漫画レベルでは高度な画像表現には適さない。建築設計仕様の精密なスケッチ画では動的立体感がなく説得力に欠ける。

97　第三章　運命を生きる──廣島復元事業への決意

悩んだ末に好機が訪れた。たいして期待もせずに観た話題の映画「スターウォーズ」（ジョージ・ルーカス監督）での驚くほどスムーズなロボットの動き。これは当時世に出たばかりの「3DCG（三次元コンピュータ・グラフィックス）」によるものとわかった。この手法を何とか応用できないだろうか。

当時、国内の建築設計事務所が「パース（完成予想図）」に代わる新しいプレゼンテーションのツールとして「3DCG」の導入を始めていた。私は伝手を頼って、当時話題を呼んだ岩国の錦帯橋をCGで描いた建設業者との連携に成功した。大正時代の建築雑誌に産業奨励館の基本設計図が掲載されていることがわかり、それを参考に精密なCG画像の作成に取りかかった。

産業奨励館だけではなくその周辺の町並みや家屋の風景も必要だ。町や通りの復元には欠かせない地図も作成した。町並み復元の参考資料として全国六十か所以上の「伝統的町並保存地域」をくまなくめぐって調査をした。あらゆる角度からデジタル写真を

98

撮影しその数は三万枚を上回った。京都や奈良、金沢、近江八幡、飛騨高山など、戦災を免れた地方都市の古い町並みは、被爆以前の廣島の面影と似かよい、ＣＧ画像づくりに大きく役立った。

私のこの作品では「一次情報」を典拠とすることを基本理念とした。当時を知る製作者、つまり私自身が記憶と体験を生かして総指揮をとる。さらに当時を知る元住人や被爆生存者を探しだし、直接会ってあらゆる角度から徹底的に体験の聞き取りを行う。

そして、その証言からストーリーを構成し、さらに実証映像としてリアルで高度なＣＧ画像を作成する。

人間の記憶をつなぎ合わせながら記録写真や文書資料などからの検証を加えて、かつてあった「廣島」という「場」を再現させる。つまり在りし日の「ふるさと」を再びよみがえらせるのだ。私は奇をてらわず記録映画の基本や本質を忠実に実践する手法をとった。

生き残った住人や当時町内の職場で働いていた人々の捜索を始め、記憶を頼りにかつての町内の人々に連絡を試みた。その結果、子ども時代

99　第三章　運命を生きる――廣島復元事業への決意

に記憶のある思いもかけない人々が生き残っていることもわかった。中には昔、親しみを込めて「おじさん、おばさん、お兄ちゃん、お姉ちゃん」と呼んでいた人たちもいた。「無事に生きておられたのか。」思わず懐かしさと嬉しさが湧き上がったこともしばしば。

この事業構想を知った地元のNHK広島放送局や中国新聞社などが取材を兼ねて協力を申し出た。全国規模で爆心地ゆかりの人々の捜索が始まり、その結果じつに北海道から九州や沖縄までの各地で百六十五名もの関係者を探しあてることができた。その中には当時産業奨励館で働いていた七名も含まれている。

当初の予想では、これほどまでに多くの人々を探しだすことなど到底できないと思われた。事業が進むにつれて新聞やテレビでの報道も全国規模へと拡大、情報収集における報道メディアの底力をまざまざと見せつけられた。

人づてに元の住民や生存者の輪は次第に広がっていった。隣近所、遊び仲間、同じ学校、子供会、町内会、稽古事の同好、お寺の信者、行き

つけの店や理髪店での顔なじみ……。それぞれが記憶をたどり思わぬ人々に繋がっていった。

北海道の伊達市から沖縄の那覇市まで各地に赴き、自分の足と目で丹念に聞き取り調査を行った。

当時を知る元の町民たちと会って、最初に口にされる言葉は「ほんとに田邉の息子さんが生きていたの！ 奨励館の隣で家族全員亡くなられたと思っていたのに！ よう生きとったねぇ！」

まじまじと私の顔を見てしばらくは感慨にふけるばかりであった。

こうして多くの人々からたくさ

元住人が集まり復元事業を立ち上げ

101　第三章　運命を生きる――廣島復元事業への決意

んの貴重な証言を得た。長い時間が過ぎているにもかかわらず故郷のたたずまいや原爆体験に関する記憶は、いずれも昨日のことのように鮮明であった。

質問はなるべく簡略に、しかも淡々と世間話をするように打ち解けてから行った。質問項目は予め限定して、いずれも高齢者であることから面接時間は六十分を上限とした。また、聞き取りの趣旨と質問項目、答えたくなければ答えなくてよいことも事前に通知しておいた。内容が内容だけになるべく精神的な負担をかけないように心掛けたつもりだ。

忘れることができないそれぞれのつらい思い出。途中で絶句したり嗚咽(おえつ)を漏らし私ももらい泣きを繰り返した。あまりのことに聞き取りを中断したこともあった。

一人一人を訪ねて全国各地でかけがえのない証言収録作業を続けた。「こんなことを続けていいのだろうか。」これは本当につらい仕事でもあった。しばしば心が折れそうにもなった。

これまでに一度も自身の被爆体験について話したことのない人も少な

くなかった。この事態は同じ体験をした者でないと決してわからない、理解ができないことと思う。

最終的に八十六名もの方々から聞き取りを行うことができた。高齢により記憶が薄れていたり、体調を崩して入院していたり、認知症が進んでいる証言者も多く、時期としてはまさにぎりぎりであったことを痛感した。

聞き取りによる情報をもとに、それらを裏付ける科学的な精査と分析を重ねた。広島の被爆史の中で、これまで半世紀にわ

元住人から聴き取り調査と証言収録

第三章　運命を生きる——廣島復元事業への決意

たって埋もれていた在りし日の爆心地の全貌が、薄紙をはぐように明らかになっていった。

実証に必要な被爆前後の広島の記録写真を探す目的で、全国の資料館や公文書館、図書館などに問い合わせた。

しかしながら非協力的な対応をされることが多く作業は困難を極めた。東京の国立施設では「何に使うのか、簡単には見せられない、どうしてもというのなら、（複雑な）手続きをせよ。」というありさまである。日本の関連施設はなぜ不作為で無用な役人風を吹かし、かくも煩雑で不親切なのだろうか。

そうこうするうちに、原爆に関する記録写真や映画フィルムなど貴重な資料が大量にアメリカにあることを知った。

——果たして原爆投下の当事国から重要な資料や情報提供の協力が得られるだろうか。

半信半疑で渡米した私をワシントン郊外にあるアメリカ国立公文書館の学芸員は温かく迎え協力してくれた。彼らは「ヒロシマから、さぞ長

104

い旅だったことだろう。」
とねぎらい、労を惜しまず親切丁寧に関連資料の検索方法や保管場所を教えてくれた。

そこで見つけ出したファイルには何れも「極秘」と刻印され、初めて目にする写真も多かった。すでに見たことがあるものでも原版プリントのため実に鮮明であった。その一枚一枚から不明だった情報も数多く抽出でき、多くの貴重な資料を入手することができた。

ワシントン米議会図書館

驚いたことに被爆以前の廣島や戦時中の日本の生活風俗に関する写真も数多く存在し、私は慄然とせざるを得なかった。戦時中、アメリカはこれほどまでに敵国日本に関する大量の情報を入手していたのだ。

なかでも原爆投下数日前の廣島市全域の航空写真を入手していた時には恐怖を覚えた。拡大してみると我が家の物干しに布団が干してある様子まで手に取るようにわかる。さらに驚くべきことには、戦時中の日本の生活風習をカラー映画に収録したフィルムさえあった。町家や商家の店先、台所での食事の準備、普通の家庭の食事風景、布団を敷いて寝るところや子どもたちの三輪車遊びまで、当時の生活の断片が十六ミリ映画に鮮明に収められていたのである。アメリカ軍は廣島の地理はおろか、市民生活の細部まですべて正確に把握していたのだ。

――情報だけでもすさまじい彼我の相違がある、こんな大国強国を相手に無謀な戦争をさせられたのか。――こんな不毛な戦争に巻き込まれ、その結果敗れた父親たちの無念は如何ばかりであったか。空疎な「神風」や「大和魂」で戦争をするような相手ではなかったのだ。

アメリカでの情報収集は訪れるたびに新たな発掘があった。国立公文書館へは前後五回、ワシントンのアメリカ議会図書館へ二回、さらに海軍省歴史資料館や大学図書館などからも爆心地復元事業をより確実にするおびただしい実証写真資料が入手できた。いずれも証言や記憶を裏付けるとともに原爆の実態を明確にするものばかりだった。

こうした苦労の末に爆心地の復元事業は成った。第

米海軍省歴史資料館でヒロシマ資料を発見

一作の『原爆ドームと消えた街並み』ハイビジョン映像作品は八十三分にまとめ上げた。

「ヒロシマ」を携え国連本部へ

世界遺産に登録されながらも、破壊以前の姿がほとんど確認できなかった原爆ドーム、その全貌を証言とハイテク画像で再現できた本作は国内のみならず広く海外からも注目を浴びた。

NHK広島放送局のハイビジョンホールで行われた完成披露試写会には多くの関係者が訪れた。私の中学時代の同級生たちも現れ、代表から花束を受け取ったときは胸が熱くなった。私のもっともつらかった時代を知っている彼らである。

上映が終わってから見知らぬお年寄りから話しかけられた。

「この世で再び、産業奨励館や懐かしい町が観られるとは思いませんでした。ありがとう、冥土への土産にします｡」

108

完成試写会には多くの観客が訪れた

109　第三章　運命を生きる——廣島復元事業への決意

かつての廣島の姿を知る人でなければ出てこない言葉であった。どの褒め言葉よりも嬉しく、この仕事をして本当によかったと自分に言い聞かせた。

だが各方面から賞賛を受けるかたわら、私の中では次第に何か空しい気持ちが募っていった。

原爆ドームは確かに復元した。しかしもっと周辺の町の様子を描き、そこにあった普通の市民の暮らしを再現したかった。町に漂っていた「空気」とでも言えようか。何よりも、そこに生きていた人々の息遣いや体温、存在の痕跡を描きたかった。

私は作品完成の余韻にひたる間もなく、第二作のわが町「爆心地猿楽町復元」に取り掛かった。

この作品のコンセプトは前作で成し得なかった「生活者の視点で描く」ということだった。

猿楽町企画は「原爆ドーム編」で手掛けた戸別地図だけで、各戸の見取り図もなければ詳細な資料もない。まるまるひとつの町を復元するの

である。事業規模は膨大となり製作費を含めて一〇零細企業で取り組める規模では到底なかった。基本的には原爆投下糾弾と非人間性がテーマとなり、その性格や主張の内容から民間ファンドや公的な支援助成など期待できない。しかしながら生存者の高齢化が進んでいることから作業は急を要する。

やむなく製作に必要な事業資金を個人保証で銀行から借り入れ、見切り発車でスタートせざるを得なかった。

第一作の経験から、この事業はさらに社会的な影響が大きいことがわかっている。歴史に残る実証記録作品として成果への責任も重くのしかかり、より専門的な知識も必要だった。ナック映像センターを主幹社として産官学連携による製作委員会方式を採用することとした。

「産」は事業の総括推進を受け持ち、直接製作に携わるわが社と高い志のある地元の映像事業者、高い技術力を持つCGクリエイター、そして中核的な立場で情報提供と協力支援を行う「矢倉会（爆心地生存者の会）」の代表メンバーで構成する。

「官」は原爆関連の情報を収集し提供する広島平和文化センター、技術支援で広島産業振興センターなど広島市の外郭団体が協力した。

「学」はＣＧ画像生成など視覚効果の技術開発を進める、地元の広島市立大学芸術学部と情報科学部、わが国の伝統的町並みの保存研究を手掛ける広島工業大学の建築工学部など。

これ以降、新たな作品ごとに同様の委員会体制を敷くことにした。やがてＣＧ描写や表現技術も発達して先進専門分野の大学を交えた製作体制が確立されるようになった。

さらにアメリカの最先端大学の協力も得て、技術的には充実した環境でシリーズ作品を次々に完成させることができた。

二〇〇〇年（平成十二年）、爆心地復元シリーズの初作品『原爆ドームと消えた街並み』を携えてニューヨークの国連本部を訪れた。スクリーンを前に国連スタッフは驚きとともに目を見張った。ヒロシマの爆心地には被爆以前にはどんな町があり、どんな町家や商家があり、どんな人々がどんな暮らしを営んでいたのか。彼らが初めて見る映像がそこにあっ

ニューヨークの国連本部ビル

第三章　運命を生きる――廣島復元事業への決意

た。これがきっかけとなり、以降国連との親密な交流が始まった。

一方、いつも苦労させられたのは膨大な事業費の調達だった。国や地方自治体にわずかな公的支援や助成を求め、作品完成後のテレビ放映などの映像使用権料、画像使用の著作権料を見越して銀行に追加融資を求める以外に方策はない。

民間企業からの支援はとても期待できない。地元には、原爆被災の原因ともなった太平洋戦争の戦時特需や被爆後の復興事業、さらに朝鮮戦争景気でも利益を上げて成長した企業も少なくないが、この「国際平和貢献」事業に援助を申し出る企業は一社もなかった。

こんなこともあった。地元経済界の会合で代表的企業のトップから言われたことがある。「立派な仕事をしておられる、何か当社でお力になれることがあれば──」。

真に受けて、後日その会社を訪ね事業費の窮状(きゅうじょう)を訴えたところ、担当から返事があった。「誠に申し訳ないのですが、原爆関連事業はわが社には馴染みませんので──」。国際平和文化都市を標榜する「広島」の

現実である。

　苦しい台所事情を知っている親しい友人たちはあきれて私に尋ねる。「なぜそんなに苦労してまで、復元事業に余生と情熱を賭けるのか——。」

　答えはいつも同じである。「自分がやらなければ誰がするのか」と。

　ヒロシマ爆心地の復元作業を決意してからの十四年。それは膨大な事業費の調達に奔走し、ひたすら映像製作に取り組み、それまで誰も手掛けていない、手掛けることが出来なかっ

国連軍縮担当に作品DVDを寄贈

115　第三章　運命を生きる——廣島復元事業への決意

た歴史的な事業。それは苦労の連続であったが、さまざまな人々の温かい声援に恵まれた歳月でもあった。私はこの長い時間をかけて、ついに「原爆」に関するライフワークを世に問うことができた。

『原爆ドームと消えた街並み』
『爆心地猿楽町復元〜ヒロシマの記憶〜』
『ヒロシマ・グラウンド・ゼロ〜あの日、そこでは何が〜』
『爆心地／総集編〜ヒロシマの記録〜』
『ヒロシマからの伝言〜原爆で失ったもの〜』

の五作品がそれである。すべて還暦六十歳を過ぎてからの仕事であった。

若い頃の私は、原爆をテーマにライフワークとしての映像作品を作るなど夢にも思っていなかった。今、振り返ってみると、原爆と訣別した五十年におよぶ空白の歳月は決して無意味ではなかった。長い時を経て、ようやく原爆を総括的にしかも客観視することができるようになり、冷静な目で情報の分析ができるようになった。そして、

国連会場でテレビ取材に応じる筆者

何よりも自分自身の中で「原爆」へと立ち向かうエネルギーを蓄積できた。私がこれらの作品を手掛けることは必然であり運命でもあったのだ。今はそんな気がしている。

第四章　ヒロシマからのメッセージ
～次の世代への伝承～

私の願う「平和」

「自分はたびたびヒロシマを訪れている。そのたびに思うのだが、爆心地の対岸が公園でよかった。あの場所が公園でなかったら、被害はもっと大きかったはずだから。」

この驚くべき発言をしたのは、アメリカのジャーナリストだった。二〇〇七年（平成十九年）、ニューヨーク国連本部のプレスルームで「爆心地／総集編」を上映した時のことである。

上映後のインタビューでの出来事だった。瞬間、私はわが耳を疑い、訂正と反論をせずにはいられなかった。

「その認識は間違っている」、被爆以前の平和公園は「中島」と呼ばれ、広島有数の繁華街であり、あの日にも多くの一般市民が普段通りの朝を迎えていた。朝食のあと片付け、掃除や洗濯、植木への水やり、仏壇参り、水遊び……。そんな日常生活を送る人々の上空六百メートルで、あ

120

の忌まわしい原子爆弾は炸裂したのだと。

その記者は、私の渾身の訴えに驚き息をのんだ。やがて彼は言った。

「そのことこそ訴求力がある。世界中の人々が訪れている原爆慰霊碑や資料館のある平和公園、そこがかつては繁華街で市民生活があったという事実を、是非とも伝えてはどうか。」

その帰路の飛行機の中で、私は彼の言葉が頭から離れなかった。――

「確かに。」

壊滅的な被害にあった爆心地の対岸、中島の町は、もはや公園にする

広島有数の繁華街中島地区／現在の平和記念公園（CG画像）

以外になす術がなかったのである。一家が全滅した世帯も多く、土地の権利確認も区画の整理や再現も不可能だった。そして、そんな酷い事実を彼らは知らなかった。想像もしていなかったことだろう。

いや、アメリカ人の彼だけではない。日本人の中にも、広島市民ですら知らない人はたくさんいるに違いない。

彼と同じく、あの場所が以前から公園だったと誤解していても責められない。しかし、私にとっては決してあってはならない誤解である。

幼い頃、私は母や祖母に連れられて、よく川向こうの中島へ行った。中島はいつも賑わっていた。おもちゃ屋、菓子屋、下駄屋、お茶屋、紙屋、海産物屋、洋品店、眼鏡店、映画館……。どれも私の住む町、猿楽町（さるがく）にはなかった店々である。

父の後について料亭や旅館にも行った。父は軍の同僚や部下と中島によく出かけていた。料亭の女将（おかみ）さんからお菓子をもらうのが私の楽しみだった。紙包みを大切に抱えながら、この形はせんべいだろうか、それ

ともビスケットだろうか、金平糖（こんぺいとう）や黒糖飴も入っているかも、わくわくしながらひとり帰りの相生橋を渡ったものだった。

私は決意した。次の作品は中島地区を取り上げよう。爆心地の対岸、中島地区の復元事業の中であらためて気づいたことがあった。今生きている被爆経験者は、そのほとんどが当時は少年や少女だったということである。私同様に突然訪れた家族との離別や生活環境の破壊――。

期せずして幼い身で苛酷（かこく）な環境へ投げ出された彼らは、その後どのように生き延びたのだろうか。親の愛情や庇護を幼い日に突然失うことがどれほどつらいことか。

私は再び精力的に聞き取り調査を行い、中島地区の復元を進めていった。五ヶ町からなる中島地区の調査は難渋を極め、製作には実に三年を要した。そしてそれが最新作『ヒロシマからの伝言』として結実した。

二〇一〇年（平成二十二年）九月のことである。

エジプトでの訴え

その年の五月、ニューヨークの国連本部で「NPT（核不拡散条約）再検討会議」が開かれた。

この時、外務省の公的後援により、NPT関連行事で上映とスピーチをすることができた。

本会議初日の昼休みとあって、会場にはNPT参加の各国代表をはじめ、国連ジャーナリストやアメリカ在住の被爆者、地元大学の関係者や国連職員らが訪れた。彼らはみな、高精細ハイビジョンで映し出される在りし日の廣島に見入っていた。

スクリーンの中では、現在の平和公園の場所に、CGでよみがえらせた京都や金沢のような伝統的な町並みが現出していた。土蔵を構え木造づくりの落ち着いた町家と商家が軒を連ねている。料亭や旅館、寺院、銭湯、理髪店、映画館、洋食堂、呉服屋……。私たちの思い出の中に生

き続けている情景が、鮮明に映し出されてゆく。

自身の被爆体験を語るシーンになると、頬がゆがみ涙する生存者の表情に、観客は固唾(かたず)を飲んでいた。そして語られる被爆直後のヒロシマ。江戸時代に城下町として開け、明治、大正、昭和へと発展を続けた伝統的な街並みは、あの瞬間に跡形もなく消え去った。

公園の地面深くには、今も行方不明者として五千人を上回る遺体が埋まっている。わずかに原形を留め、あるいは高熱で粉末状になった遺骨が瓦礫(がれき)とともに散乱し眠っている。

上映後の講演で私は訴えた。

「広島の平和の象徴として、多くの人々が平和公園を訪れる。靴を脱げとは言わないが、せめて歩いている地面の下に今も犠牲者が眠っていることを知ってほしい、感じてほしい。その原因を思い起こし、再びあってはならない戦争の傷跡をしっかりとかみしめて頂きたい。せめて公園をそっと歩き、慰霊の気持ちを忘れないでほしい。」

この前後には、ニューヨークのコロンビア大学やロサンゼルスの南カ

ルフォルニア大学、カルフォルニア州立大学でも同様の催しを行った。大学生を中心とした若い世代が熱心に聞き入り、率直な質問を受けた。何よりも彼らが注目したのは、一般市民が巻き込まれ、その多くが犠牲になったという事実であった。

この時、難しい質問も受けた。質問者はコロンビア大学の教授で、遠慮がちに彼はこう聞いた。

「——被爆者として生き残った人と犠牲になった人、原爆により生と死を分けたのは何だったのか。」

しばらく考えたが、この時の私には「運命」としか答えざるを得なかった。あの日あの時、爆心地にいたのか、いなかったのか。私の母と弟はまさにあの日の午前中に、広島を発つはずだった。偶然、爆心地にいた人もいるし、たまたま広島から離れていた人も多かっただろう。

しかし今となっては、あの答えは誤りだったと思う。原子爆弾を開発し、投下したのは紛れもなく「人間」ではないか。あ

の許されざる行為による殺戮(さつりく)を「運命」として受け入れるべきではない。決して「運命」として受け入れるわけには断じていかない。

こんなこともあった。

二〇一〇年（平成二十二年）十月、私は日本政府の非核特使として中東のクウェートとエジプトを訪問した。国際交流基金の海外事業である。核戦争の火種がくすぶる地域のせいか「原爆を体験した人」として興味を持って迎えられた。各地で爆心地の記録映画の上映と講演を繰り返したが、この地でも、やはり原爆に対する知識は極めて希薄であるように思えた。

この時のカイロ会場でのエピソードである。上映と講演を終えた後の質疑応答で現地の知識人から質問を受けた。

「当時の日本は軍国主義国家であった。原爆の投下により戦争の終結が早まり、結果的に多くの人命が救われたのではないか。」

いわゆる「原爆正当論」である。私は強い口調で反論した。

「原爆に正当論などあり得ない。」

「原爆投下、それ自体が非人道的な犯罪行為であり、いかなる理由をつけようとも、被爆者として、それを容認することは絶対にできない。」
　その発言が通訳された瞬間、会場から大きい拍手が沸き起こった。その時、私は遥かなるエジプトの地で深い感銘を覚えた。国境、民族、人種、宗教を超えて「真実」は受け入れられる。勇気をもって伝えることだ。
　ヒロシマからのメッセージをあらゆる国の人々に伝えなくてはならない、そのことこそ原爆から生き残った者の使命であり役割でもある、と。
　私は「平和運動家」でもなく、「反核」を職業とするものでもない。一被爆者、一市民、一映像作家の立場で、自らの信条にもとづいて記録映画製作に携わっている。そしてその作品を通じて、国内をはじめ海外へ向けて〝ヒロシマを二度と繰り返してはならない〟と訴えかけているつもりである。

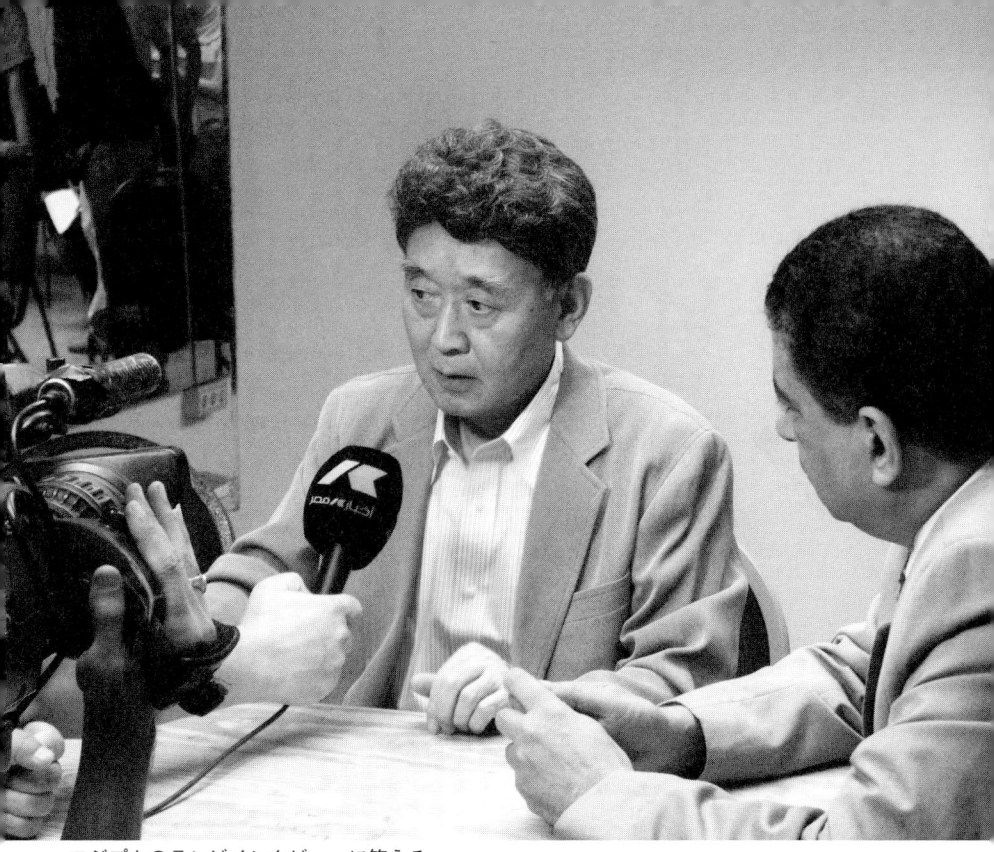

エジプトのテレビインタビューに答える

エジプト・カイロにて記者会見に臨む筆者　　カイロ会場のメディア

第四章　ヒロシマからのメッセージ～次の世代への伝承～

静かに届ける平和の心

私は「平和運動」という言葉を聞くと、つい身構えてしまう。かつて、少年時代に手記「原爆の子」をめぐって、大人たちから酷い目にあった記憶がそうさせるのだろう。平和への純粋な思いが踏みにじられ、信じたものに裏切られた。その背景の多くは「平和運動」にあったのだ。

被爆者の心情としては、八月六日はそっと静かに迎えたい、というのが本当のところである。亡くなった肉親を悼み、心から供養し祈りを捧げたい。

ところが毎年全国から「平和運動家」が大勢押し寄せ、終日にわたって騒音をまき散らす。こともあろうに「ダイ・イン」と称して、原爆ドームのそばで横たわるデモンストレーションまでする。地下で眠る犠牲者たちは、さぞや嘆いていることだろう。

130

「自分たちの犠牲は、何だったのだろうか。」と。
ドーム近くの菩提寺に参っても、騒音がうるさくて手を合わせることすらできない。両耳を押さえながら手を合わせることができるだろうか。心ない「平和活動家」に言う。「あの日はヒロシマへ来ないでくれ、そっとしておいてほしい。」というのが被爆者の〝声なき声〟、正直なところだ。

平和祈念式典にしても、その参加者や来場者は自覚しているのだろうか。自分の足元に行方不明者として、今も多くの人々が遺骨のままで眠り、原形をとどめあるいは粉骨状となって踏みつけられているという現実を。

あの日、あの場所──中島では、十四歳前後の中学生や女学生たちが早朝から建物疎開に駆り出され、暑い日差しの下で汗を流していた。そして、裸同然あるいは薄手のシャツ姿で懸命に作業をしていた。そこへ何の予告もなく、突然五千度を上回る灼熱が襲いかかり、幼さが残る身体を焼きつくした。

あの一帯にいた多くの人々が、普通の市民が、あの瞬間に地獄を体験

第四章　ヒロシマからのメッセージ〜次の世代への伝承〜

しながらこの世を後にした。平和公園への来訪者はそのことをしっかりと心に刻んでほしい。敬虔（けいけん）な祈りの気持ちで地面をそっと踏んでほしい。

私にとっての「平和」は、ひとことで言えば「安穏」である。「心安らかで穏やかな社会環境、その中で人間は人間として価値ある日常を過ごす」ということである。そして、そこから何かが見え、悟り、人への思いやり、社会生活における共存や協調、さらに生きることへの本来の意味を知る。

「平和運動」にもいろいろな形がある。

二〇一〇年（平成二十二年）五月、南カリフォルニア大学で爆心地復元映画の上映と講演を行った時のことだ。学内に「ショア（ユダヤ語で虐殺の意）」と呼ばれるラボ（研究施設）があった。あまりにもむごたらしい戦争の傷跡と体験を忘れないために、ホロコーストの実態を記録し解明する研究財団がそこにあるのだという。

訪問してみると、財団の創始者はかの映画製作者で監督のスティーブン・スピルバーグ氏であった。急な訪問でさすがに監督に会うことはで

きなかったが、広島から来たことを告げると、スタッフがそのラボの目的や業務を詳細に説明してくれた。

私の「爆心地復元プロジェクト」と彼らの事業が似通っているのは、体験者からの直接的ヒアリング調査に最大の主軸を置いている点である。ドイツやポーランドのみならず、ヨーロッパ全土を中心に、世界各国から五万人を上回る証言を集めて分析を行っていた。

虐殺から生き延びた人々や犠牲者の家族をはじめ、「殺し」「殺された」立場が違う双方から、音声収録やビデオ映像で証言を記録している。

多部門でアカデミー賞を獲得した映画「シンドラーのリスト」を製作したスピルバーグ監督も、自らのユダヤ系の出自から執念とともに事業に取り組んでいる。その理念は、まぎれもなく〝あの悲劇を再び繰り返してはならない〟という人類共通の平和への希求であった。

そのラボには、スピルバーグ監督の名声や財団の国際的な規模により、世界中から賛同の募金が集まっている。私から見ると羨ましいほどの巨額の予算で財団は運営されていた。私が「ヒロシマ・プロジェクト」で

133　第四章　ヒロシマからのメッセージ〜次の世代への伝承〜

は、事業の財源はほとんどが個人の持ち出しであることを打ちあけると、なぜ国や地方が支援や助成をしないのか、なぜ寄付が集まらないのか、スタッフは首をかしげていた。

そして、日本の社会全体が原爆を忘却し風化しつつある中で、三百人を超える証言収録を独力で行った私たちの取り組みに、彼らは賞賛を惜しまなかった。二十世紀の負の遺産である「ヒロシマの原爆」と「ユダヤ・ホロコースト」──。彼らとはお互いに平和な世界の実現をめざして、今後連携協力を深めようと約束をした。

私は思う。真の「平和運動」とは拳を振り上げて、処構わず相手かまわず、大声で喚き散らすことではない。ほんとうは、静かに穏やかに人の心に訴えるものではないかと。活動家が唱えるような「戦って平和を勝ち取る」というスタイルは、どうも馴染まないように思えて仕方がない。

仏教でいう「安穏」への思いこそが、真の平和への願いに近いのではないだろうか。

被爆から七十年へ──新たなる決意

還暦を機に始まった私のライフワークは、第五作『ヒロシマからの伝言、～原爆で失ったもの～』で、プロジェクトとしての幕引きを考えていた。

自分はなぜこの世に生を受けたのか、何のためにこれまで生き延びてきたのか、そして何をして人生を終えるべきか。

自問自答をする中で、出来ることなら「世の中のために、人のために」役に立つ仕事で終えたい、自分として「やるべき仕事を成し遂げて、両親が待つあの世へ行こう」と結論付けた。

映像製作の仕事は、地道でひたむきな作業の連続である。作品の規模が大きくなればなるほど内容や成果が問われ、当然ながら個性的な創作力や実行力、製作過程においては統率力や判断力、テーマ表現への情念と冷静さを使い分け、想像を超える知的エネルギーを必要とする。

「映画製作の旬の年齢は六十歳代前後」と私には断言できる。世界に名だたる名匠でも、高齢や晩年の作品には秀作がほとんどない。老いの哀れさだけが残りいずれも駄作で晩節を汚す例が少なくない。一方、三十代や四十代では人間としての未熟さ、人格形成への途上にあり問題外。真の映画づくりにおいては、「はなたれ小僧」の域を出ない。彼らが作る浅薄で稚拙な駄作愚作を見るにつけ、もっと自分自身を磨いてからにしてほしい。劇映画で言うならば、観賞料金に程遠いものばかりである。

かく言う私も、いたずらに馬齢を重ねたに過ぎないが、自分の生きる道として修業を積み重ね、同時に人一倍健康に気を付けて生きてきた。おかげで気力も体力も精神力や創造力も、まだ枯れてはいない。もう一度だけ最後の挑戦がしたい――。自身の内面からそんな誘惑の声が聞こえてくる。

記録映画の本質は「人間の、経験を積んだ作家の視点を通じて主題を描く」ということである。これは私の哲学理念であり人生観でもある。

証言収録の筆者（左）

そして、そこに意味を求めるならば、多少の「老い」は許されるかもしれない。情熱で何処までカバーできるか、神仏の加護を頼みながらも、私はファイナル・プロジェクト（最終の仕事）に踏み出した。

記録映画『爆心地半径一キロ以内の復元〜ヒロシマの真実〜』は、被爆七十周年（二〇一五年）の記念事業をめざしている。

被爆体験者は著しく高齢化している。その時期にあって、一次情報はおそらくこれで「終幕」ともいうべき役割を担うことになるだろう。

本作で対象となる地域は、原爆ドームを爆心地として、東は八丁堀の福屋百貨店、南は国泰寺町の広島市役所、西は天満川、北は軍事施設に囲まれた広島城界隈の範囲。

被爆以前には、この圏域に廣島の政治、経済、文化、市民生活のすべてがあった。

作品の構成は、これまでのシリーズと同様に、証言者からの聞き取りによる一次情報がベースである。記録写真や高度なCG画像で実証しながら、被爆以前の町並みや目抜き通り、商店街や民家の並び、主だった

建物や施設を可能な限り忠実に蘇生再現させるつもりである。

私の記憶にあるこの地域は、城下町の面影を色濃く残す「職能町」でもあった。伝統的な町名について、祖母や町の物知りから教わってそれぞれの意味を知った。少年時代に地域の歴史を学んだものだ。

猿楽町、細工町、紙屋町、研屋町、鉄砲町、針屋町、革屋町、塩屋町、鳥屋町、西魚屋町、鉄砲屋町、材木町、木挽町、水主町、鍛冶屋町、左官町、蟹屋町、猫屋町、西大工町、鷹匠町、寺町……。

いずれも町名が、在りし日の面影や風情を彷彿とさせる。戦後の無味乾燥な町名の簡素化で、惜しくも消え去ってしまった地名も多い。

現在の広島を見て「見事な復興」という人がいるが、私はそうは思わない。かつての廣島、良き時代の廣島は原爆で破壊され消滅した。そしてその後、完全に新しい町として造り替わってしまっただけ――。

これが私の認識である。

被爆以前の町のたたずまい、そこに住む人々の生きよう、地域を思う心意気や誇り、歴史や伝統文化を大切に受け継いでこそ真の復興ではな

139　第四章　ヒロシマからのメッセージ〜次の世代への伝承〜

いか。新しい町づくりや何の変哲もない建物を作っただけでは「復興」とはいえない。

現在、市街地のメインストリートは、東西に貫く相生通りであるが、この通りは城下町の時代には広島城の外堀であった。明治時代に埋め立てられて市内電車が開通した。

ほぼ中心の紙屋町からは南の宇品港とを結ぶ路線、八丁堀には北方の東練兵場方面への分岐線があり、路線の拡充に沿って次第に都市機能が発展していった。

電車道を挟んで町はさらに開け、とくに八丁堀界隈は栄えた。百貨店（現在のデパート）ができ、南に隣接して賑やかな金座街、そのすぐ近くには新天地の歓楽街があった。

その辺りでは芝居小屋や劇場、映画館など娯楽施設と大小の商店が混然一体となって賑わいを見せた。今ほどいろいろな娯楽がない時代、人々は繁華街に集まり買い物や非日常を楽しんでいた。

私が子どもの頃、両親や祖母に連れられて革屋町から本通り、八丁堀

140

方面へ行くのがたまらなく嬉しかったものだ。いつも心がときめいていたものだ。地域この付近では原爆により多くの老舗の店主や経営者が亡くなった。地域の文化や伝統を身をもって支えた「町の大人衆」（地域を先導する真のリーダー）が根こそぎ犠牲となった。

今では、もはやすっかり味もそっけもない何処にでもある町に成り下がっている。繁華街特有のわくわくする雰囲気や地域の伝統文化もなく、これといった魅力はまったくない。当時の心のときめきの片鱗すら感じられず、全国どこへ行っても見られる平凡な商店街になってしまった。

それだけに、被爆以前の町の復元は重要である。人の温もりや息遣い、町や通りに漂っていた風情や人情、商人の心意気や気風、それに応える粋な客たち。訪れるときの期待感、そして帰る時の満足感がとても懐かしい。

これらは、いずれも「まちづくり、賑わいづくり」の原点である。町の「復興」に際して"忘れられ、失われた大切なもの"があることを知ってほしい、ぜひとも思い出してほしいものだ。

また、私は本作品の重要なシーンとして、爆心地の北東に広がっていた軍事施設を、その実態とともに鮮明に描き出したいと考えている。これまでその存在は知られていないながら、行政も報道や言論界も封印し黙殺してきた背景がある。

そのことは、軍事施設として明確に取り上げるならば、原爆投下直後からアメリカが主張する「軍事施設を目標に原爆攻撃をした」という姑息な言い訳に結びつき、迎合する恐れがあったからであろう。

確かに爆心地の北東に、帝国陸軍の師団司令部など中枢機能は置かれていた。しかし、そこにあったのは軍司令部のほかには司令官の官舎や陸軍病院、被服倉庫、輜重隊（しちょうたい）（物資の調達や保管の業務）、通信隊、教育隊、憲兵隊、陸軍が経営する学校などであった。重武装による強力兵器の配置や攻撃型の実戦部隊ではなく、実態は後方支援が主たる任務である。

証言によると、あの日にも当該地域には、おびただしい数の入院療養中の傷病兵、戦地への配属を待つ将兵の野営など、実質的には「非戦闘

員」が大半を占めていたという。

また、軍事施設の大半を占める東と西の練兵場は「市民との共有の場」でもあった。とくに西練兵場においては、広場に面する護国神社を中心に春秋の大祭や季節行事、大相撲広島場所の巡業、神楽や能楽の奉納などが行われていた。

練兵場の広場では、博覧会、競馬、オートバイ競争、サーカス、市民運動会も頻繁(ひんぱん)に開催され、一般市民の利用が絶えなかった。師団司令部の置かれた広島城界隈でも、私たち子どもは、お堀端で遊んだり、トンボを追っかけたり、食用蛙の釣りを楽しんでいた。あの日も練兵場の入り口、神社の大鳥居付近では、銃後を守る町内会の婦人連がモンペ姿で消火訓練のバケツリレーを行っていた。

原爆投下の言い訳として「軍事施設を爆撃したもので、そこには一般市民はいなかった。」は、もはや通用しない。

長い歳月が「真実」を解明することがある。今だからこそ見えてきたこともある。歴史の襞(ひだ)の中で読み解き知らねばならないものもある。そ

143　第四章　ヒロシマからのメッセージ〜次の世代への伝承〜

れらは時代を超えて、とても大切なものではないかと思う。そして、そのことこそ、これから挑戦する復元事業の重要な基本構想でもある。

ヒロシマとフクシマ

原爆投下という「許すべからざる非道な行為」――。

あれから半世紀以上も過ぎた日本で、核を介して再び同じことが繰り返されるとは思いもしなかった。

原爆により大切な家族と生活のすべてを失い、途方に暮れていた少年時代。持って行き場のない恨みや憤り、悲嘆の日々が片時も頭から離れない。

「原爆さえなかったら」そう思わぬ日はなかった。

小学校の社会科教科書の「原子力の平和利用」という文字が目に留まった。核エネルギーを応用して、発電のみならず、豊かな暮らしに関わるあらゆる分野で有効に利用できるとあった。

「これだ！」少年の心に灯がともった。当時の思いや切なる願望は、被爆体験手記「原爆の子」にも明確に記している。

「ピカッと光って、大音響がすると同時に広島市は全滅してしまった。こんなすごい災難を人間がうけたことがあろうか。（略）原子力はおそろしい、悪いことに使えば人類はほろびてしまう。でも、よいことに使えば使うほど人間が幸福になり、平和がおとずれてくるだろう。（略）最後に、原子力を悪い方面でなくて良い方面に平和のために使用できることを祈る。」

希望を抱き、心をこめて書いたつもりであった。以来、この思いを自身の心の糧として生きてきた。出てきたときには光明を感じた。その後も水爆をふくむ核兵器の保有国（アメリカ・イギリス・フランス・ロシア・中国）がこぞって原発を推進していることを知り、不条理を感じながらも希望を抱いたものだ。

しかし、その裏側では、不毛な戦争と同様に、原発利権をめぐる巨悪の構造が着々と拡大していようとは——。

「原子力の平和利用」という、かつて生きるために自分へ言い聞かせ祈るような思い。それはもはや根底から裏切られ覆されてしまった。原爆と同様に「核の平和利用」など、あり得なかったのである。

今となっては、少年時代この方、虚偽の安全神話を信じ切った自らの不明を恥じるとともに、腹立たしく情けなく愧怩たる思いである。そして、またもや裏切られたことへの持って行き場のない怒りを抑えることができない。

原発に関わる連中には、人間としての良心や道徳はおろか「善悪の区別」さえつかないのだろうか。

コンプライアンス（企業倫理）が著しく欠如した「東京電力」を主体として、企業献金や集票に群がる政界、既得権益と天下り確保に奔走する省庁や官僚、膨大な利権や事業費の取得争奪に血道を上げる業界や財界、安全神話の画策や研究開発費の支援助成依存の学会、巨額な原発交付金取得で自治努力を忘れ地域財政を賄う地方自治体、想像を超える広報宣伝費で口を封じられたマスコミ報道機関……。

146

その醜態は日に日に明白となっている。

何れも「金」にまつわる浅ましい巨悪の構造であり、「原子力電源立地」を舞台に繰り広げられた天をも怖れぬ悪辣非道な所業である。

ヒロシマとフクシマの実態を目にした今、「核の平和利用などあり得ない」と結論せざるを得ない。戦争であれ原発であれ、それを保有管理するのは、ほかならぬ「人間」であるからだ。

戦乱や災害に際して「人間」がしばしば正常な判断力を欠き、守るべき責任をはじめ正義や良心の欠如をもたらすこと。時に倫理観を忘れ、自己の利益のためならいかなる手段や犯罪的行為をもいとわない。それらは六十数年前のヒロシマで白日の下にさらされ、そしてまた、フクシマにおいて救いのない悲劇が再演されたのである。

これから何年、いや何十年も続く原発クライシス。社会不安や人体への影響を含めて、ヒロシマの例を見るまでもなく、事態の「収束」などあり得ない。

原発利権の構造はさらに「真実」を隠蔽し、早くも国家補償や電力料

147　第四章　ヒロシマからのメッセージ〜次の世代への伝承〜

金の値上げなど姑息で言語道断な謀略を画策している。許されざる権勢の盛衰と末路はすでにはるか昔、人の世の常として「平家物語」が図らずも説いている。

「祇園精舎の鐘の声、諸行無常の響きあり。娑羅双樹の花の色、盛者必衰の理をあらはす。おごれる人も久しからず、唯春の夜の夢のごとし。たけき者も遂にはほろびぬ、偏に風の前の塵に同じ。」

そして私は怒りを込めて糾弾する。「撒いた種は自分で刈り取れ、恥を知れ」と。

平和を願う世界の人々へ——遺言

手元に数枚の写真がある。二〇〇七年（平成十九年）、四度目の渡米調査で、アメリカ国立公文書館において入手した写真である。

この写真を見た時の衝撃はあまりにも大きかった。涙がとめどなく溢れ、まるでその日は仕事にならなかった。これまでに原爆の直撃で炭化

148

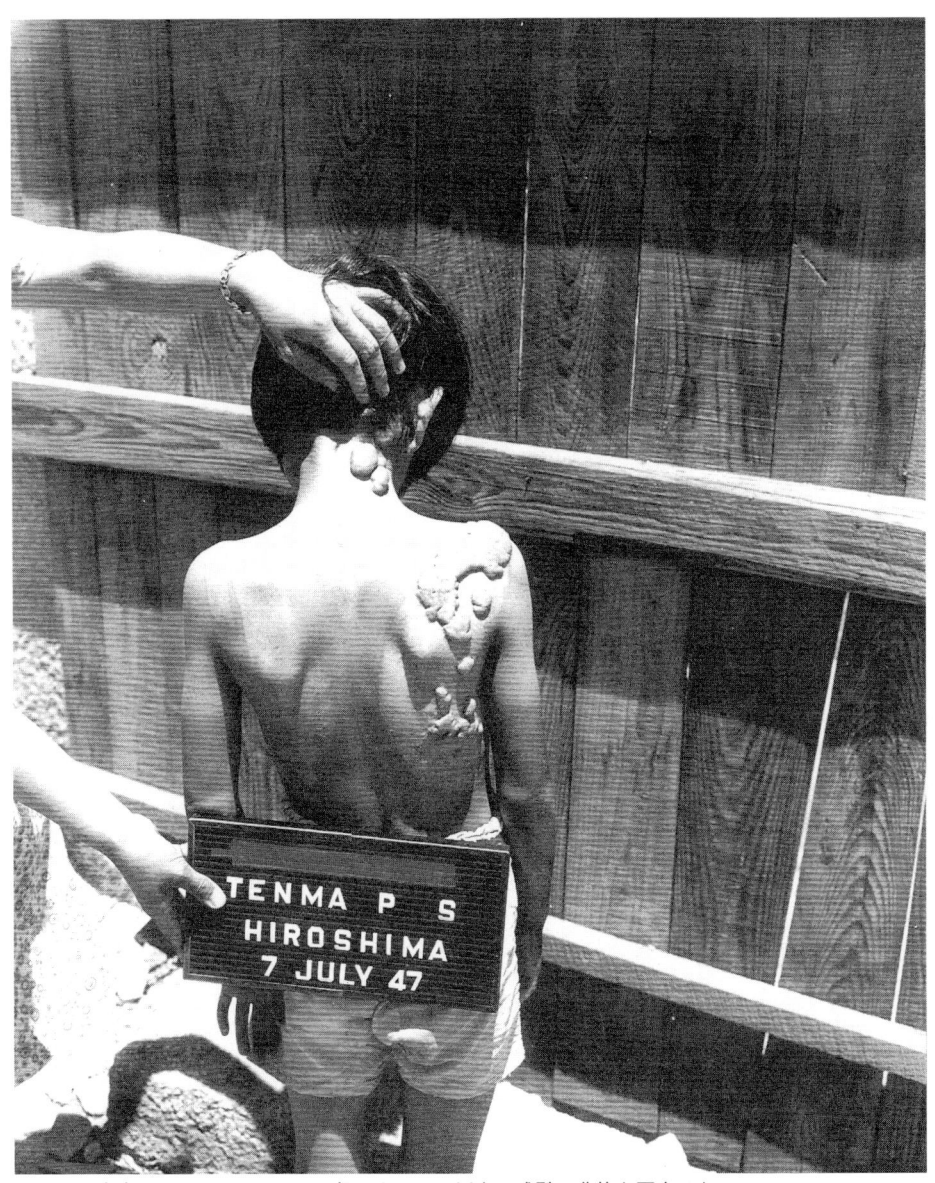

少女をモルモットのように扱った、これ以上の残酷で悲惨な写真はない

第四章　ヒロシマからのメッセージ〜次の世代への伝承〜

した無残な遺体、目を背けたくなる人体被災のケロイド写真は数多く目にしてきた。しかし、これより陰惨なものはなかった。
残念ながらこの写真は、記録映画「爆心地復元シリーズ」のテーマには馴染まないので、今日までこの写真を公表せずにずっとファイルの中に眠らせていた。
あまりにも残酷な写真ゆえ甚だ逡巡(しゅんじゅん)したが、勇断をもってここに掲載することにした。この写真を隠したまま、あの世へ行くことはとてもできない。
原爆投下から二年後の記録。この写真の少女は被爆時には国民学校の高学年(十一歳)。原爆を浴びた稚い背中には、すでに肉腫が盛り上がり余命は明らかである。私がこの写真を見た瞬間に激しい怒りを覚えたのは、仕事柄この写真撮影現場の状況が推測できたからだ。
撮影のために、少女の上半身の裸を晒(さら)したばかりか、被爆場所の校庭で記録用のボードを入れ込み、アングルを指図している……。思わず言葉にならない怒りがこみ上げた。

150

この少年はあとどのくらい生き延びただろうか
子どもまでもモルモットとして扱う戦争の非道

「人間としての良心はないのか！　おまえたちには家族はいないのか！」

これはとても人間の所業とは思えない。撮影したカメラマンや立ち会った人間らに、良心の欠片（かけら）でもあるのだろうか。人間の生命への畏敬（いけい）や尊厳はないのか。これと同じことを自分の家族にできるのか！

戦争の恐ろしさが此処にある。そこでは、被写体の少女たちはモルモット以外の何物でもない。この場所に立ち会う人間たちは、罪の意識が麻痺していたことだろう。「戦勝」の名のもとに驕り高ぶり、残虐性に酔いしれたに違いない。

そして今、原爆の悲劇を、もうひとつ明らかにする。

『原爆の子』の手記にN君の名前がある。N君は私より二歳年下で「原爆の子友の会」でも一緒に活動をしていた。彼は爆心地から二キロ地点の吉島で被爆。原爆で両親を奪われ、おばあさんと二人だけが生き残った。私と同じような境遇でもあり弟のように思っていた。いつも明るく笑顔を絶やさず快活な少年だった。

その後、私は「友の会」活動に愛想をつかし、さらに原爆の地に訣別して山口県へ引っ越してしまった。以来N君とも音信が途切れていた。それから数年がたち、風の便りに彼が広島市郊外の精神障害者療養施設に入院していることを知った。

見舞いに訪れると、彼はまるで人が変わっていた。あの頃の面影はまったくなく明るさや笑顔もなかった。虚ろな表情でわずかに反応するばかりである。

N君が『原爆の子』に寄せた手記の一部である。

「──ぼくが時々町へ出て行くと、よくお父さんお母さんに手をひかれている子供を見かけます。幸福そうに楽しそうにあるいている子供……。うらやましく思います。(略)ぼくは今は、おばあちゃんの家でそだっている。これもみんなせんそうがあったためだ。広島市をやいたのもせんそうのためだ……。」

──これこそ、「原爆の子」の率直な心からの叫びである。

付き添いのおばあさんに聞くと「親がいない寂しさやつらさから、だ

153　第四章　ヒロシマからのメッセージ〜次の世代への伝承〜

んだん人が変わっていった」という。私と二歳の差は存外に大きかった。何とか窮地から這い上がった私と違い、N君は被爆時にたった六歳――。厳しくつらい環境に自ら抗うことができなかったのだろう。こうしたこととは、実際に体験した者でなければ決してわかるまい。

当時、高校生の自分には何もできず、気にしながらも時は過ぎて行った。大学時代、帰郷した折にも行方を訊ねたがずじまいに終わった。その後、新聞社に勤務していた頃になってやっと見つけることができた。

N君は地元の自動車会社の下請け企業に入り、工場の床掃除などの雑役に従事していた。私の顔を見るなり「田邉くん！」という。昔は、二歳上の私を「くん」などと呼んだことはなかったので、一瞬不審に思いはしたものの名前を覚えていてくれたことは嬉しかった。

私は彼の手を見て驚いた。まだ二十代だというのにゴツゴツと節くれだち、まるで老人のような手であった。思わず彼の手を握りしめ涙が抑えられなかった。まぎれもなくその手には想像に余りある彼の苦悩の

明るく快活だったN君(左)と筆者

日々が刻印されていた。

彼は友の会活動や私との思い出をほとんど失っていた。唯一の肉親のおばあさんもすでに亡くなっていた。ぽつりぽつりと話す中で彼はふと漏らした。「楽しいことなど、何もありません──。」私には返す言葉がなかった。

数年前にもN君に再会した。その時、彼は直接被爆による癌を発病して入院療養をしていた。躁鬱症状もあり目が離せない状況であった。「友の会」の会長だったNさんも、誰に言うでもなく被爆者手帳や生活援護手当の取得に奔走し、不遇なN君を支えていた。

私にできることは、ときどきそっと枕元に見舞い金を置いたり「食べたい」というケーキを届けたり、下着や着替えの衣類を差し入れる程度のことだった。彼の生活費はわずかな年金と被爆者健康手当だけ。生活保護制度や被爆者養護施設への入所が適応できないものか、現在掛けあっているところである。

今、七十歳を過ぎた「原爆孤老」N君の境遇を思うとき「何が彼をそ

うさせたのか。」と思わずにはいられない。深い孤独の中で心の病を患い、まともな仕事にも就けず、家庭も持てず、子どもにも縁がない生涯——。

原爆のせいで陽の当たることのなかった人生。

アパートの一室で、「いつも、ひとりぼっちの暮らし」彼は何を思い孤独な日々を過ごしてきたのだろうか……。

私たちは知るべきだ。人間でありながら人間としての営みができない人生があったことを。そのような現実を目の前にして、改めて原爆の憎むべき惨禍（さんか）を直視しなければならない。人間として目を背けてはならない。

日本国憲法の第十三条に、生命の安全、自由および「幸福追求」に対する国民の権利が規定されている。N君は、まぎれもなく日本国民の一人である。被爆後の彼の長い人生に「幸福」のこの字でもあったのか。

周りを見渡すと「平和」を訴えて、あまたの「平和運動」が盛んである。高邁な理想を掲げた未来志向の運動も必要かもしれない。しかしながら、目の前の「不幸せ」を黙殺した「苛酷（かこく）な現実」を放

置し続ける世相には、率直に疑問を感じる。

不幸のどん底にある孤老のN君一人を救えない平和運動に何の意味があるのか。せめて薄幸な人生の終盤において、わずかな「幸福の片鱗（へんりん）」でも与えることはできないものか。せめて『原爆の子』の印税の一部なりとも、彼に与えられれば……。原著記述寄稿者の立場で、ことあるごとに「原爆の子基金」の設立を提唱するが、反応はおろか実現の気配はまったくない。

先日、N君とともに彼のご先祖とおばあさんが眠る、広島デルタを見下ろす山の端の墓地にお参りした。杖を頼りに近づく変わり果てたN君を前に、泉下のご家族はどう思われたことだろうか。

これまでに手掛けた爆心地復元事業を通じて、全国で三百人以上の方々から聞き取り調査を行った。その一人ひとりが重い荷を背負って半世紀以上を生き延びてきた。その証言はたとえようもなく重い。

「あの日、大切なものをすべて失った、その後の人生はいばらの道だっ

「原爆は、何の罪もない女、子どもや年寄りまでも殺し尽くした」

「何の予告もなく、逃げるとまもなく、多くの生命が奪われた」

「長い年月を癌や白血病と闘いながら、かろうじて生きている」

「持っていき場のない怒りや憎しみを、どこへ向ければいいのか」

「戦争では何も解決しない。憎悪が残るだけだ」

「次に戦争が起これば、人類は間違いなく破滅する」

「原爆投下への正当論は認められず、私たちには残酷だ」

「非道な当事者に対して、許すことを考えるべきなのか」

「被爆者は、核兵器の恐ろしさを伝える以外に、他にすべきことはないのだろうか」

「ささやかな幸福な日々を、一発の原子爆弾は、すべてを破壊しつくした」

「いつも思う、原爆さえなかったら──」

彼のアーネスト・ヘミングウェイは言っている。

「いかに必要であったとしても、いかに正当な理由があったとしても、戦争が犯罪だということを忘れてはならない。」

これにならって私は言おう。

いかに必要であったとしても、いかに正当な理由があったとしても、原子爆弾の投下は、許すことのできない「極悪非道な国際犯罪行為」であったと。

あとがき

　ご縁とは不思議なものである。
　二〇一〇年の春、第三文明社から爆心地復元映像の上映と講演の依頼がありお引き受けした。それがご縁となり、この度同社より拙著の刊行をして頂くことになった。
　これまで誰も手掛けることが出来なかった、爆心地情報の空白については『ぼくの家はここにあった』(文藝春秋刊)に詳しく記述し、ヒロシマの実態研究や全国の学校教育現場における平和教育の学習教材として幅広く活用されている。
　小著については、激動の昭和時代を生き抜いた一人として、とくに少年時代の不毛な戦争体験や苛酷な原爆体験を通じて〝原爆の惨禍が再びあってはならない〟との願いを込めた「少年Tの昭和」として記述する

構想を、私はかねてから抱いていた。

出版企画段階において、本書の内容を広く海外にも啓発し伝達していきたいという意図から、英語訳併記構想が持ちあがった。そこでタイトルや内容についても協議の結果、世界の人々に理解しやすく『少年Tの昭和』から『「少年T」のヒロシマ』へと改めた。英文が併記されることで国際的視野を目指す情報発信版となった。

筆者は、爆心地に生まれ育ち原爆の惨禍を体験し、その後「映像作家」の道一筋に歩み、半世紀に及ぶ「被爆体験との断絶」を経て、還暦を機に自分にしかできない宿命的な仕事を見つけ出した。

人生終盤のライフワークと位置付け、十数年の歳月をかけて映像による爆心地復元事業に取り組んだ結果、これまでに五作品を完成させることが出来た。そして今、映像人生の総括事業として「爆心地半径一キロ以内の復元」への挑戦を開始したところである。読者の中で関連情報や当時の写真をお持ちの方は、どうか協力して頂きたい。

爆心地における生き残りの一人として"やるべきこと"を成し遂げた

いと願っている。わが故郷「爆心地」へのこだわりを背景に、これまで精魂込めて取り組んできたが、史上初のプロジェクトだけに、達成感とともに重い責任を感じ続けてきた。

一次情報による実体験の証言をもとに、高度なＣＧ画像による描写や当時の音の再現などが高い評価を頂く一方、映像表現の限界も感じ忸怩(じくじ)たる思いを抱いている。

ありし日のしっとりとした町並み、そこに暮らす人々の息づかい、和やかな人情、街角から漂う臭いなど記憶に残る町の空気をよみがえらすことは、到底できないことにも気が付いた。

いかに努力をしても復元不可能なもの、それが「原爆によって失ったもの」そのものである。

ここまで出来たのは神仏のご加護以外の何物でもない。

長い人生の中では、行き詰まったり挫折に陥り絶望の淵に立った時も多く、その都度救いの手を差しのべ、勇気をもって困難に立ち向かう「ちから」を授けられた。人智を超えるものの存在を、あるいはそれに

対する敬虔な祈りの意味を知らねばならない。そこから生まれる自立心や自助努力、それなくして今日の自分はなかった。

信仰とは〝よく生き、よく終えるための道しるべ〟というのが今の私の宗教観である。

小著が多くの人々に読まれ「ヒロシマの真実」を伝え、読者ご自身のこととして実態を理解され、そのことを周りの人に伝えて頂く。そこから人類社会に核廃絶の輪が広がればこれに勝る喜びはない。

爆心地における被爆生存者として、映像作家冥利とともに、来る日には心置きなくあの世へ旅立ちたい。

末尾ながら、本書の出版に惜しみないご協力を頂いた各位に心からの敬意と感謝を申し上げたい。

ありがとうございました。

合　掌

二〇一二年一月

著　者

【追　記】

　本書の写真およびＣＧ画像は、著者が構成し製作した下記の記録映画からその一部を活用した。
　『原爆ドームと消えた街並み』『爆心地猿楽町復元』『ヒロシマ・グラウンド・ゼロ』『ヒロシマからの伝言』。
　プロジェクトの達成をめざす復元事業を通じて、写真の提供者には心から感謝を申し上げる。
　被爆前後の写真の所蔵および提供は、米国立公文書館、米議会図書館、米海軍省歴史資料館、英国立公文書館、広島平和文化センター、広島市公文書館、広島市文化振興課、毎日新聞社、被爆生存者、爆心地の元住人などである。　英文翻訳の監修は、ヒロシマの事情に詳しく、実績が豊富な著者の友人でもある、小泉直子さんに依頼した。さらに、英訳の文体が適切で、より分かりやすく理解されるよう、広島在住の、エリザベ

ス・ボールドウィン、スティーブ・リーパーご夫婦にも、献身的な協力をして頂いた。
挿絵は岡崎佐和子さんである。
諸機関や団体および諸氏のご協力のおかげで、内容をさらに充実することができた。重ねてお礼を述べたい。
――ありがとうございました。

①平和を訴える世界遺産の原爆ドーム　②ありし日の産業奨励館、広島市物産共進会の時の電飾　①The World Heritage A-Bomb Dome, symbol of our pledge to work for peace　②The Industrial Promotion Hall, illuminated for a local product exhibition

原爆ドーム

③廣島のシンボルだった産業奨励館
④産業奨励館で働いていたタイピストたち
⑤産業奨励館の内部、貿易会社の事務所
③The Industrial Promotion Hall, symbol of Hiroshima
④Typists who worked at the Industrial Promotion Hall
⑤A trading company office in the Industrial Promotion Hall

④

⑤

169　原爆ドーム

⑦

⑥

⑧

⑥なごやかな戦前の市民生活　⑦中島本通りの化粧品卸屋、特別大売出し
⑧被爆以前の本通り商店街　⑨被爆以前の廣島駅　⑩被爆以前の廣島中心部、右上に産業奨励館

⑥ The friendly ambience of the neighborhood before the war　⑦ Sale at a cosmetics wholesaler on Nakajima Main Street　⑧ Hondori (Main Street) before the bombing　⑨ Hiroshima Station before the bombing　⑩ Central Hiroshima before the bombing (Industrial Promotion Hall at the upper right)

⑨

⑩

171　ありし日の廣島　人々の営み

⑪被爆以前の中島中心部（現在の平和公園）
⑫被爆後の産業奨励館内庭、翌々年瓦礫の中に若芽を見つける

⑪Central Nakajima before the bombing (current Peace Memorial Park)　⑫The courtyard of the former Industrial Promotion Hall; two years after the bombing, young buds sprout midst the debris.

⑬にぎわう護国神社境内での祭り行列　⑭元安川の夏、天然のプールとしてにぎわった

⑬Lively festival procession at Gokoku Shrine　⑭Summer fun at the Motoyasu River – a natural "swimming pool"

173　ありし日の廣島　人々の営み

⑮猿楽町の家並み、はるかに産業奨励館（ＣＧ画像）　⑯細工町から産業奨励館（ＣＧ画像）　⑮ A street lined with houses in Sarugaku-cho, with the Industrial Promotion Hall in the background (CG image)　⑯ The Industrial Promotion Hall seen from Saiku-machi (CG image)

⑰左に郵便局、寺院の右には産業奨励館（ＣＧ画像）　⑱細工町からの産業奨励館、正面に西蓮寺の山門（ＣＧ画像）　⑰ Post office on the left; Sairenji Temple in the middle; the Industrial Promotion Hall on the right (CG image)　⑱ The Industrial Promotion Hall viewed from Saiku-machi, with the two-storied gate of Sairenji Temple in the center (CG image)

⑲

⑳

㉑

⑲細工町通り、角に郵便局（ＣＧ画像）⑳産業奨励館、対岸の中島と本川小学校（ＣＧ画像）㉑細工町通り、正面には電車通り（ＣＧ画像）

⑲ Post office on the corner of Saiku-machi Street (CG image)
⑳ The Industrial Promotion Hall facing Nakajima across the river and Honkawa Elementary School on the far bank (CG image)
㉑ Saiku-machi Street crossing the wide streetcar street (CG image); streetcar track in the distance (CG image)

〔当日朝の再現〕
㉒縁側で針仕事(再現画像) ㉓女の子のお手玉遊び(再現画像) ㉔台所での片付け(再現画像)

[Re-enactments of the morning of August 6]
㉒ Sewing on a veranda (Re-enactment)
㉓ Girls juggling beanbags (Re-enactment)
㉔ Cleaning up in the kitchen (Re-enactment)

㉗

㉕相生橋から分流する本川（左側）と元安川
㉖中島本通りのにぎわい（現在の平和公園）　㉗原爆投下目標となった相生橋のＴ字部分　㉘焼失を続ける市街地

㉕Honkawa River (left) and Motoyasu River branching off at Aioi Bridge　㉖Bustling Nakajima Main Street (in what is now Peace Memorial Park)　㉗The T-junction of Aioi Bridge—target of the A-bomb　㉘The city engulfed in flames

㉘

㉙

㉚

180

㉙中島に残骸をさらす藤井商事ビル、遠方に産業奨励館
㉚爆心地の破壊消滅状況（米軍撮影）
㉛直後の爆心地一帯、川を隔てて中島（現在の平和公園）

㉙ The remains of Fujii Mercantile Firm in Nakajima; the ruined Industrial Promotion Hall in the distance
㉚ Total destruction at the hypocenter (Photographed by the U.S. Army)
㉛ The area around the hypocenter; Nakajima across the river (current Peace Memorial Park)

㉛

㉜直後の爆心地、猿楽町、細工町の焼失状況　㉝被爆直後の原爆ドームと元安川　㉜The hypocenter area after the bombing; Sarugaku-cho and Saiku-machi reduced to ashes　㉝The A-Bomb Dome and Motoyasu River after the bombing

㉞被爆直後の爆心地界隈　㉟すべて焼失した廣島城天守閣と一帯の軍施設　㉞The hypocenter area after the bombing　㉟The tower of Hiroshima Castle and Japanese Army facilities burned to ashes

8月6日原爆投下

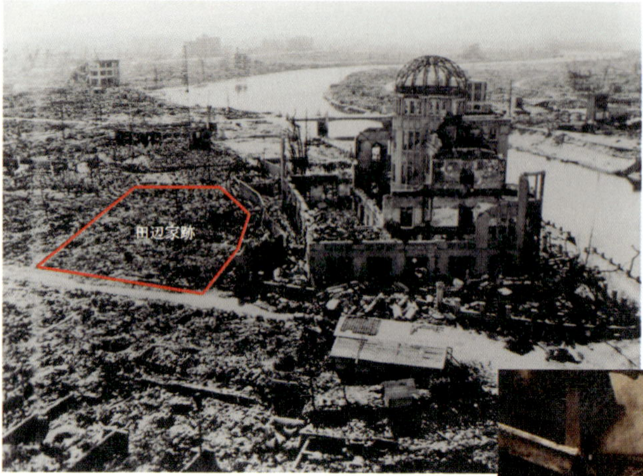

㊲

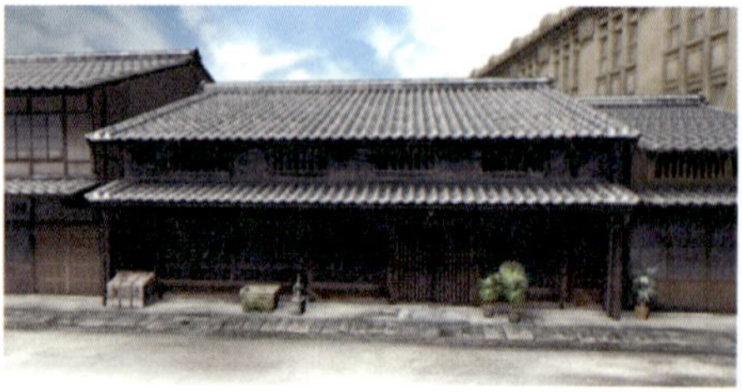

㊳

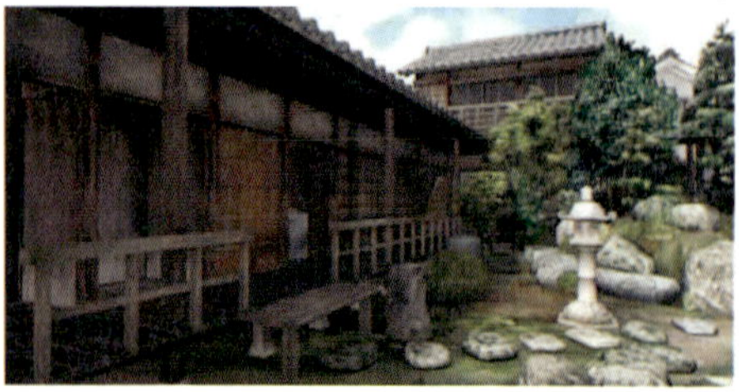

㊴

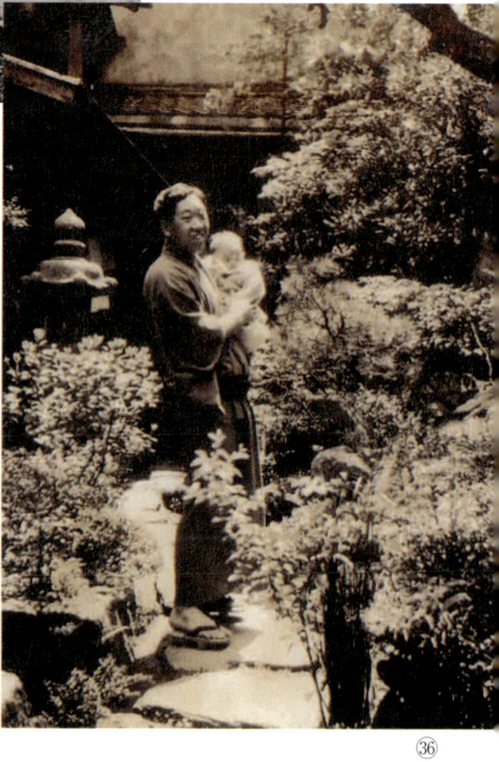

㊱

㊱庭で父に抱かれる弟、後方に石灯籠と土蔵　㊲原爆ドーム東隣りには筆者の屋敷跡〔筆者の家屋敷ＣＧ画像〕㊳格子戸の土蔵造り、右手に産業奨励館　㊴屋敷の庭、縁側がめぐり離れ座敷や土蔵があった　㊵筆者５歳、植え込みの中に後日盗難にあう石灯籠　㊶母の茶道お点前

㊱My father holding my younger brother; stone lantern and our storehouse behind　㊲Where my house stood, east of the A-Bomb Dome　㊳My house with its lattice facade; the Industrial Promotion Hall on the right (CG image)　㊴The garden facing our veranda, with the annex and the storehouse beyond (CG image)　㊵Myself at age five; behind me stands the stone lantern that was later stolen　㊶My mother performing a tea ceremony

185　田邉家と原爆

平和都市・ヒロシマの象徴として、訪れる人々に平和の尊さを訴える「原爆ドーム」
The A-Bomb Dome, a symbol of peace for those who visit Hiroshima—the City of Peace

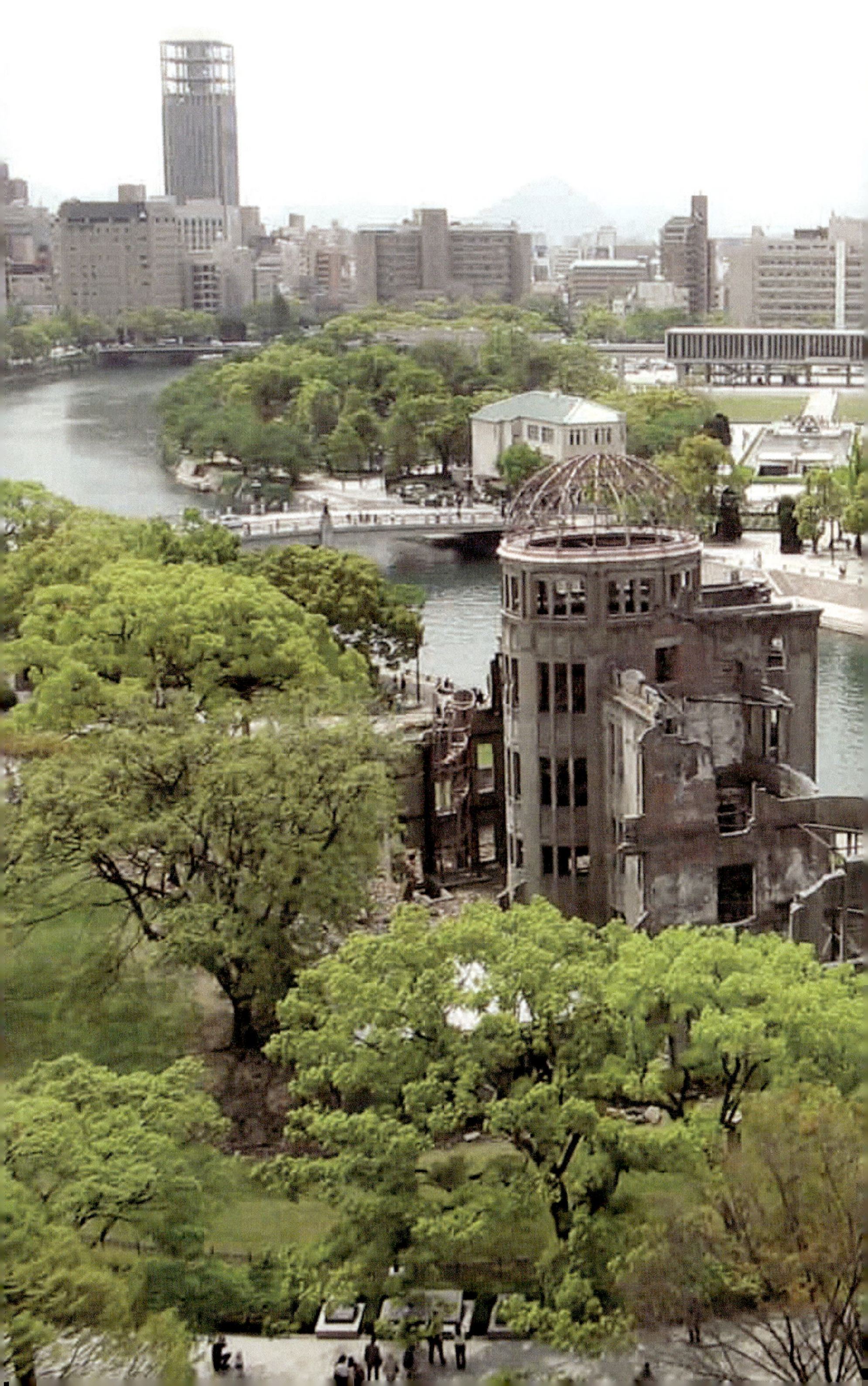

and Records Administration; the U.S. Library of Congress; the National Museum of the U.S. Navy; the National Archives (U.K.); the Hiroshima Peace Culture Foundation; the Hiroshima Municipal Archives; the Cultural Promotion Division of the City of Hiroshima; the Mainichi Newspapers Co., Ltd; survivors of the A-bomb; and former residents of the hypocenter.

The illustrations in the book are by Sawako Okazaki.

I asked my friend Naoko Koizumi to supervise the English translation. She has a deep understanding of Hiroshima and understands what I wanted to convey in this book and the background of my projects. I also asked Elizabeth Baldwin and Steve Leeper to assist with the editing. Thanks to their dedication, the book has been properly translated, and my message is clearly conveyed.

All the institutes, organizations and individuals mentioned have enriched the content through their cooperation, and I am very grateful.

Thank you.

all my heart, I thank everyone involved in the publication of this book.

Thank you.

January 2012
With my palms pressed together,
Masaaki Tanabe

Postscript

The photographs and the CG images used in this book have been adopted from the following documentary films:

The A-Bomb Dome and the Vanished City; *The Restoration of the Hypocenter Sarugaku-cho—The Memory of Hiroshima*; *Hiroshima Ground Zero—August 6, at the Hypocenter*; *Ground Zero—Documents of Hiroshima*; and *An Unrecognized Loss—Message from Hiroshima*.

I am profoundly grateful to all those who gave me permission to use photographs. The photographs of Hiroshima before the A-bomb were provided by the U.S. National Archives

Epilogue

While I have received very positive feedback, I keenly feel the limits of what can be communicated by images alone. In that sense, I'm not satisfied with my works.

It's impossible to recreate the genteel atmosphere of the town that existed, the heartbeat of the residents, their kindness, and the scents of the neighborhoods. No matter how hard I try, certain *things* cannot be recreated; these *things* have been lost forever because of the A-bomb.

Whatever I have accomplished, I owe to the protection of the gods and the Buddha. During my long life, many times I came to a dead end and felt desperate. They always extended a helping hand and gave me the energy to face the difficulties with courage. It's important to believe in a power that transcends the human mind and to pray reverently to that being. My beliefs have supported my development of a spirit of independence and self-reliance. Without them, I would not be what I am. Religion is a guide that helps you know how to live your life and end it well.

Through this book, I wish to convey truths about Hiroshima. I hope that readers make what happened here their own and convey the message to people around them. Nothing could give me greater joy than helping to expand the network of people working for the abolition of nuclear weapons.

As a survivor born at ground zero and a filmmaker, when the time comes, I will go to the world beyond with no regrets. With

suggestion was also made to change its title from *The Showa Period of Boy T* to *Born at Ground Zero—Speaking the Truth from Hiroshima* to indicate more clearly what the book is about. The publishing of this book in both Japanese and English will greatly expand its reach.

I was born near the hypocenter and experienced the horrors of the A-bomb. Having survived this tragedy, I single-mindedly pursued my career as a documentary filmmaker. After severing myself from my A-bomb experience for more than half a century, I turned 60 and finally found my true calling, my mission.

As the lifework of my latter years, I dedicated myself for more than a decade to recreating the area around the hypocenter in films. I have made five such films. Now I have embarked on my final work, *Reconstructing a Radius of One Kilometer from the Hypocenter—The Truth of Hiroshima*. If any of you readers have any information or photographs of this area before the bombing, I would greatly appreciate your cooperation.

As a survivor from the hypocenter community, I earnestly wish to finish what I feel I must do. Focusing on my hometown, I have put my all into the unprecedented project of reviving lost neighborhoods in film. I have felt a heavy responsibility as well as much fulfillment.

The information conveyed in my films is based on firsthand testimonies of those who know this area. We used state-of-the-art CG imaging to render the scenes and reproduce the sounds.

Epilogue

It's interesting how we encounter people in life. In the spring of 2010, I was asked by the Daisanbunmei-sha publishing house to lecture and show my film on the reconstruction of the hypocenter area. That led to Daisanbunmei-sha publishing this book.

In my previous works, *This Is Where My House Was* (a DVD book; Asahi Shimbun Publications, Inc.) and *The Hiroshima That Was Destroyed by the A-Bomb* (Bungei Shunju, Ltd.), I tried to share what I knew or had learned, in as much detail as I could muster, about the largely unknown hypocenter area. These books are being widely used by researchers on Hiroshima and as materials for peace education in schools around Japan.

In approaching the present book, as one who began life during a meaningless war, suffered the atrocity of the atom bomb as a child, and lived through the turbulent Showa Period, I initially planned to title it *The Showa Period of Boy T*. I was going to tell my story to frame my demand that the brutality of nuclear weapons never again be inflicted on anyone.

While discussing this book, the idea of translating it into English to convey its message to a wider audience came up. The

"Nothing can be solved by war. All that remains is hatred."

"If another world war occurs, humanity will perish for sure."

"Arguments to justify the bombing are far too cruel. We cannot condone them."

"Should I consider forgiving those ruthless leaders?"

"As A-bomb survivors, is there anything we can do other than convey the horrors of nuclear weapons?"

"One single atomic bomb destroyed everything about my humble but happy life."

"If only the A-bomb hadn't been dropped."

Ernest Hemingway wrote, "Never think that war, no matter how necessary, nor how justified, is not a crime." I add, "No matter how necessary or how justified, the dropping of the A-bomb was a malicious international crime that must never be condoned."

but wonder. Future-oriented campaigns with lofty ideals may be important, but how can people ignore their suffering neighbors and the circumstances that cause their misery? What meaning is there in peace movements if they cannot save a single human life like my forlorn friend? Could the final years of his desolate life permit him a glimpse of happiness? If only he could receive some portion of the royalties of *Children of the Atomic Bomb*! I have been calling for the establishment of a "Fund for Children of the Atomic Bomb," but to no avail. The idea never seems to materialize.

The other day, N and I visited the grave of his ancestors and grandmother on a hillside that overlooks the Hiroshima delta. When his family in that grave saw him, now a totally different person, walking towards them leaning on a cane, how did they feel?

In recreating the hypocenter, I interviewed more than 300 people. For over half a century after the A-bomb, each one lived a hard life. Each of their testimonies is somber.

"On that day, I lost everything that mattered. My life since has been one hardship after another."

"The A-bomb killed innocent women, children and the elderly."

"There was no warning. Many people died with no chance to flee."

"Battling cancer and leukemia for many years, I'm barely alive."

"Where should I direct my anger and hatred?"

mumblings revealed his truth. "I have never tasted happiness." I could not respond.

A couple of years ago, I again met him, now hospitalized for cancer due to direct exposure to the A-bomb. He also suffers from bipolar disorder and needs close attention. A former president of the Friendship Association had been supporting him and had applied for the *hibakusha* certificate and *hibakusha* welfare benefits on his behalf. All I could do was slip some money by his pillow, bring him underwear, clothes, and some cakes he liked.

Over 70 years old now, he lives on a tiny pension and medical allowance for *hibakusha*. I'm investigating to find out if he can apply for social aid or live in a nursing home for *hibakusha*. Why was this man condemned to live in profound loneliness and suffer from mental illness? He never had a decent job; he never knew the joy of family or children. Because of the bomb, he never had his day. Spending his life all alone in his tiny apartment, what did he think and feel?

Please know that some people have been denied the minimally decent lives that all human beings deserve. We must squarely face the miseries and sufferings that the atomic bomb has caused.

Article 13 of the Japanese Constitution stipulates that people have a "right to life, liberty and the pursuit of happiness." N is a citizen of Japan; over the long years since the A-bomb, has he known a moment of happiness?

Many call for peace. Peace movements abound. I cannot help

"After his parents died, he gradually changed. Loneliness and grief hounded him."

Though we were only two years apart, that made a huge difference. At eight years of age, I somehow managed to pick myself up, but N was only six. Such a little boy lacked the means to combat his astonishingly merciless situation. Only those with similar experiences can understand what he went through.

I was just a high school student—what could I do? Although I worried about him, years flew by without my seeing him. When I visited Hiroshima as a university student, I inquired about him, but no one seemed to know where he was.

After I got a job at the newspaper company, I finally found N. He was working for a subcontractor of a local automobile maker, doing odd jobs like cleaning factory floors. When he saw me, he called out, "Tanabe-*kun*!" I was a little surprised. Since he was two years younger, he'd never called me *kun*, which one uses to address someone younger. Still, I was happy that he remembered my name.

When I saw his hands, I was shocked. He was only in his twenties, yet he had the knobby hands of an old man. Before I knew it, I reached for them and held them tight while tears rolled down my face. Each wrinkle and knob on his hands attested to constant suffering and hardship. He hardly remembered anything about the Friendship Association or about me. His only immediate family, his grandmother, had passed away. His

When the bomb exploded, he was at home in Yoshijima, two kilometers away from the hypocenter. He lost both his parents; only he and his grandmother survived. Because of the similarity of our situations, I regarded him as my younger brother. He was a cheerful, high-spirited boy who always had a smile on his face.

As I said earlier, I got fed up with the association and wanted a clean break with the disaster area, so I moved to Yamaguchi Prefecture. I lost contact with him. Several years later, I found out that he had been hospitalized in a facility for the mentally ill in the outskirts of Hiroshima. When I visited him there, I encountered a totally different person. His cheerfulness had vanished into a blank expression. He had little to say.

Here is an excerpt from N's account in the book.

> *Sometimes when I go through the streets I see children holding the hands of their fathers and mothers. These children walking along looking so happy—when I see ones like this—I remember my father and mother in those days gone by....I am now being brought up at my grandmother's. All of this is because there was a war. It was on account of the war, too, that Hiroshima burned.* (Children of the Atomic Bomb *translated by Jean Dan and Ruth Sieben-Morgen*)

This was an honest cry from one of the *Children of the Atomic Bomb*. His grandmother, who stayed by his bedside, told me,

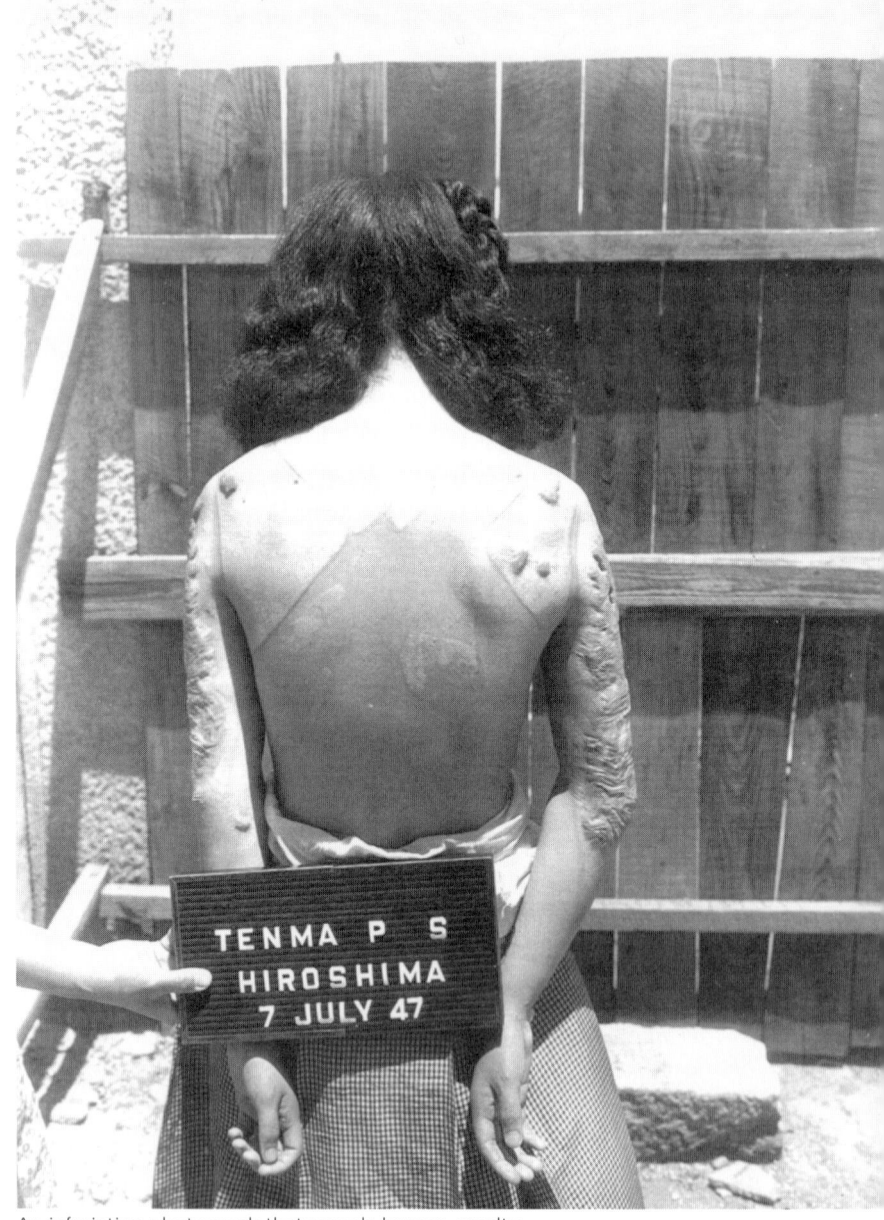

An infuriating photograph that reveals human cruelty

girls who appear in them were primary school students (11 years old) at the time of the bombing. Radiation exposure had grown sarcomas on the keloids on their backs. It is obvious that they did not live much longer. The moment I saw these photographs, intense anger welled within. Because I take photographs and films, I can easily imagine the situation in which the photographer took these shots. They were forced to expose their upper bodies in the schoolground where they were bombed, and their photographs include a signboard for the record. They were clearly told to show their scars. Words cannot express my rage. *Have you no conscience as human beings? Don't you have a family of your own?* I couldn't believe anyone could do this. Had they no respect for the sanctity or dignity of human life? Would they have done this to their own daughters?

These photographs show the horror of war. They were obviously taken to record the effects of the A-bomb on the human body. These young girls were nothing but guinea pigs. The people who shot the photographs or witnessed this probably felt no guilt. The status of "victors" must have turned these people arrogant and pitiless.

Let me enlighten the readers with one more true story about the A-bomb. One of the contributors to *Children of the Atomic Bomb* was a boy two years younger than me whom I'll call "N." We were both active members of the Children of the A-Bomb Friendship Association.

all things; the color of the sāla flowers reveals the truth that the prosperous must decline. The proud do not endure, they are like a dream on a spring night; the mighty fall at last, they are as dust before the wind. (Chapter 1.1, Helen Craig McCullough's translation)

I want to shout: "For shame! Clean up your mess!"

My Final Message
To Everyone in the World Who Hopes for Peace

On my fourth visit to the U.S. in 2007, I procured photos of A-bomb victims from the U.S. National Archives and Records Administration that shocked me terribly. That day, tears flowed ceaselessly, and I could get no work done. I had seen many hideous photos of badly charred bodies and victims with severe keloids—photos which one would normally turn away from—but none were more gruesome than these.

Unfortunately, because they were not in line with what I was trying to portray in *The Hypocenter Reconstruction Series*, I never showed these photos to the public—I kept them filed away. I hesitated to publish them in this book because they are so cruel, but eventually summoned the courage. I cannot die without revealing these photographs.

These photographs were taken two years after the A-bomb. The

gods.

Now that I have seen the reality of both Hiroshima and Fukushima, I conclude that there is no way nuclear power can be used for peaceful purposes. Whether it's for war or nuclear power generation, it is, after all, human beings who possess and control it. When faced by war or disaster, human judgment, sense of responsibility, justice and conscience all weaken. At times, morality is completely forgotten. Without hesitation, they resort to any means, even crimes, to protect their interests. This became clear in Hiroshima over 60 years ago. In Fukushima, this irredeemable tragedy is being replayed.

For decades to come, the nuclear power plant crisis will continue. One doesn't have to see Hiroshima to understand that this crisis will continue to affect society and human health. The accident in Fukushima will never be "under control."

The stakeholders of the nuclear power industry continue to hide the truth. Bailing out the company and raising electricity bills are on the table. This is how they orchestrate their cheap tricks and abominable conspiracies.

The never-to-be-condoned lust for power with its vicissitudes and its miserable end is all too common in the history of humanity. Strangely enough, the human plight is depicted in the *Tale of the Heike*:

> *The sound of the Gion Shōja bells echoes the impermanence of*

a huge evil was growing around the interests of nuclear power plants, like the evil interests of those who promote futile wars.

How I wished that nuclear power would be used for peace! This hope enabled me to live, but was completely betrayed. Just like the A-bomb, there can be no such thing as *peaceful* use of nuclear power.

Since my childhood, I fully believed the myth. I feel miserable, ashamed, and angry. How can I appease this anger? Do those in the nuclear power industry have any conscience or morals? Can they tell right from wrong?

Tokyo Electric Power Company (TEPCO) is grossly lacking in corporate ethics, but they do not work alone. Politicians flock to votes and monetary contributions from electric power companies. Ministries and agencies as well as bureaucrats busily protect their political interests and secure executive posts in private firms after retiring. The industry and the business community fight for pieces of the massive money pie. Academia advances the safety myth to secure grants to sustain their research. Local governments that host nuclear power plants depend on vast government subsidies to run their towns and villages. Fat advertising revenues from the nuclear industry induce the mass media to keep its mouth shut. Day by day, the ugly structure comes into sharper focus. Money stains the entire shameful scenario. The process of determining the location of nuclear power plants has staged acts vicious enough to defy the miserable days of fighting back bitterness, anger and sadness. Every day I thought, "If only that bomb had never been dropped."

In our elementary school social studies textbook, the words "peaceful use of nuclear power" caught my attention. It stated that nuclear power would not only generate electricity but make our lives affluent in all kinds of other ways. "Yes! This is it!" I saw a ray of hope. In sincere hope and with all my heart, I wrote what I felt at that time in *Children of the Atomic Bomb*.

> *Simultaneously with a bright flash and a stupendous roar the city of Hiroshima was totally annihilated. I wonder whether human beings have ever suffered such a disaster….Atomic power is frightful. If it is used badly the human race will become extinct. However, if it is well used, the happier humanity will be, and peace will surely come….Lastly, I pray that atomic power can be used not in a bad way but in good ways, for the purpose of peace.* (*Children of the Atomic Bomb* translated by Jean Dan and Ruth Sieben-Morgen)

Ever since, this hope has sustained me. When nuclear power generation was first introduced in Japan, I believed it heralded a brighter future. Although I felt the absurdity of the nuclear powers (the U.S., the U.K., France, Russia, China) promoting nuclear power generation while developing atomic and hydrogen bombs, I still had hope. Little did I know that behind the scenes,

events, the grand Hiroshima *sumo* tournament, Shinto dances, and Noh performances offered to the gods. Expositions, horse races, motorcycle races, circuses, and community sports events were also frequently held there. Thus, ordinary people constantly used these drill grounds.

At Hiroshima Castle, where the Divisional Headquarters was located, we used to play by the moat, catching dragonflies and bullfrogs. On August 6, at the entrance to the drill ground by the shrine gate, neighborhood association women were conducting a fire drill in their *mompe* work pants. The claim that the atomic bombing targeted an army base and not civilians is simply false.

More often than not, truth emerges over time. Certain facts become clear. But sometimes, important truths that have been buried in the course of history must be dug up. This is the underlying philosophy of the next chapter of the "reconstruction" project.

Hiroshima and Fukushima

More than half a century has passed since the unforgivable dropping of the atomic bomb. I never imagined that another nuclear disaster would occur in Japan.

When I lost my precious family and livelihood because of the A-bomb, I was devastated. I was a child. I can never forget the

remember what has been forgotten.

Depicting the military facilities located northeast of the hypocenter is a key piece of this project. I want to revive that area, what it looked like and what was actually taking place there. Although people know that military facilities were there, the government, media and the press prefer to ignore or bypass the topic. They probably fear that mentioning them would help the U.S. justify the atomic bombing with the argument that the target was an important army base.

It is true that the Imperial Army's Divisional Headquarters were located northeast of the hypocenter. In addition to the regional headquarters, there were the Commander's residence, army hospitals, warehouses, an army service unit, a communications unit, a training unit, military police headquarters and an army-run elementary school. In other words, these were rear-guard war support facilities; they did not store heavy weaponry or house combat-ready soldiers.

According to testimonies I have heard, many people even in the military headquarters area were noncombatants at that time. The hospitals were full of sick and wounded soldiers, and many of the soldiers camping there were waiting to be dispatched.

The Eastern and Western Drill Grounds, which filled a large portion of military property, were also used by the community. The Western Drill Ground, which faced Gokoku Shrine, was used for the spring and autumn festivals and other seasonal Shinto

the opening of a department store, while Kinza-gai to the south became another magnet for shoppers. The nearby Shintenchi entertainment district mixed playhouses, movie theaters and other amusement facilities with stores of all sizes. In the days before our current saturation with entertainment, people flocked to that area for shopping and its exciting atmosphere.

When I was a child, just walking with my parents and grandmother to Hatchobori by way of Kawaya-cho and Hondori (the main shopping street) was a thrill. My heart would skip at the thought. When the A-bomb killed these shopkeepers and merchants, it took the leading patrons of our culture and tradition.

Today, the area is bereft of originality and looks like any other town. Gone is the time-honored charm of the entertainment quarter; I feel no excitement there. Reconstruction has turned the whole area into run-of-the-mill streets lined with dull shops.

This is one reason it is so vital to visually recreate that area. I remember the warmth and energy of the people; the chic, courteous atmosphere; the spirited, service-minded shop owners and the quick-witted customers who bantered with them. When I recall how eager I felt "going to town" and how satisfied I was returning home, I'm overcome with nostalgia

The characteristics I describe are essential to a vital town. In the process of rebuilding, precious aspects have been forgotten and lost forever. I want people to know what was lost. I want them to

These names tell us what was going on in those quarters and hint at what it was like to be there. After the war, names were simplified with little thought. In the process, unfortunately, many were lost.

People who see Hiroshima today often say the city has been beautifully rebuilt. I disagree. My beloved Hiroshima was wiped out by the A-bomb and replaced by a completely new city. This is what I feel.

The city's distinctive atmosphere; the ways people lived; the residents' pride in and devotion to their city; its history and traditional culture—only when these aspects are respected and communicated to the next generation can one say that Hiroshima has truly recovered. How can we say a city has recovered simply because a new city with ordinary buildings is built in its place?

Aioi Avenue is the main street stretching east to west. In the Edo Period, it was the outer moat of Hiroshima Castle. During the Meiji Period, the moat was filled and replaced with a wide streetcar road.

Another streetcar line connected Kamiya-cho in the city center to Ujina Port in the south. A branch line ran north from Hatchobori to the Eastern Drill Ground. City functions developed in tandem with the extension of these streetcar lines.

The city also expanded along the streets that branched out from the streetcar rails. The Hatchobori area flourished with

Castle, the site of a former military base. This area was a center of politics, business and culture; to many, it was also home.

I approach this project as I did my previous works: interviewing witnesses to get firsthand information, then verifying it against documentary photos. I use high-definition CG images to render the cityscape, the main streets, their shops and houses, and the major buildings and facilities as authentically as possible.

I knew this area when it looked and felt like traditional craftsmen's quarters in a castle town. My grandmother and others taught me the history of the area, how the quarters had developed, and the meaning of their names.

> Sarugaku-cho (where I was born) was named after a form of Noh theater (Sarugaku)
> Saiku-cho (next to Sarugaku-cho): craftsmen, specializing in musical instruments and Noh costumes
> Kamiya-cho: paper shops
> Togiya-cho: sharpeners and polishers of swords
> Teppo-cho: gun stores
> Kawaya-cho: leather shops
> Zaimoku-cho: lumber dealers
> Shioya-cho: salt dealers
> Kajiya-cho: blacksmiths
> Takajo-machi: falconers
> Teramachi: temples

They are novices at life; in the world of filmmaking they are still green. It's hard to watch superficial, crude movies without wanting to tell the filmmakers to grow up. Immature works aren't worth the price of admission.

Looking at myself, though, I fear I have grown old with little to show for it. Still, in my own way, I have worked hard and taken extra care of my health. I'm thankful that spiritual stamina, mental and physical strength and creativity are still with me. *Give it one more shot—take on one more challenge.* These tempting words began ringing in my head.

The essence of documentary filmmaking is the pursuit of relevant themes through the filmmaker's eyes based on his or her experiences of life. This is my philosophy. If this is meaningful, then my age might not bar the way. I was unsure of the extent to which passion can compensate for advanced age, so I prayed to the gods for protection as I embarked on my final project.

The documentary *Reconstructing a Radius of One Kilometer from the Hypocenter—The Truth of Hiroshima* will be released in 2015 to commemorate the 70th anniversary of the A-bomb.

The survivors of the A-bomb are noticeably aging. Opportunities to get firsthand information from them are running out. My film targets the one-kilometer radius (from the hypocenter and the A-Bomb Dome). It reaches east to the Fukuya Department Store in Hatchobori; south to City Hall in Kokutaiji; west to the Tenma River; and north to Hiroshima

Filmmaking requires persistent effort and hard work. The larger the scale of the job, the more expectations are placed on the product. And of course, the more creativity and ability is required to get things done. In addition, you need to have leadership qualities, be decisive, have the passion to convey the theme, and yet be composed and have intellectual energy far beyond anyone's imagination.

I say with confidence that a filmmaker reaches his prime between around 60 to 70. Even the world's famous masters produce few works of genius in their senior years. Works produced in the twilight years of life tend to evidence a pathetic ineptitude that tarnishes one's reputation. At the same time, most filmmakers in their 30's or 40's are still shaping their characters.

Interviewing a *hibakusha* and recording his testimony

collected and recorded testimonies of more than 300 A-bomb survivors despite the general fading of the A-bomb experience in Japanese society. The dropping of the atomic bomb on Hiroshima and the Holocaust are bitter legacies of the 20th century. We promised each other that we would join hands in our work to realize global peace.

I believe that a true peace movement is not about raising one's fist and shouting slogans without considering time or place. It should be conducted in a peaceful manner that touches peoples' hearts. Many peace activists say we must "fight for peace," but that's not my cup of tea. I believe a true quest for peace is like the Buddhist pursuit of tranquility.

A New Resolve toward the 70th Anniversary

Initially, I thought that my fifth film, *An Unrecognized Loss—Message from Hiroshima*, would be a proper ending to my lifework, which began when I turned sixty.

I kept wondering why I came into this world, why I had survived up to now, and what my last task would be. As I asked myself these questions, I concluded that I wanted my life to end after completing some work that would contribute to people and society. I decided that I must achieve such a task before I could move onto the next life where my parents wait.

was the famous film director Steven Spielberg. Since I just happened to drop by, of course I wasn't able to meet him, but when I told the staff there that I was from Hiroshima, they welcomed me and explained in detail the purpose of the institute and its projects. My *Hypocenter Reconstruction Series* and their work both placed great importance on hearing firsthand the testimonies of those who experienced the atomic bomb or the Holocaust. They had collected and were analyzing more than 50,000 testimonies from people residing in Germany, Poland and other European countries. They made audio and video recordings of Holocaust survivors and bereaved families. They also collected testimonies from persons related to the victimizers' side. Spielberg, a Jew himself and director of the Academy Award winning film *Schindler's List*, was passionately involved in this work. He was driven by the belief that such a tragedy must never be repeated, which is humanity's shared quest for peace.

Due to Spielberg's reputation and the global scale of the foundation, donations from supporters were pouring in from around the world. I couldn't help but feel how lucky they were to have such a huge budget. When I told the staff that I had been mostly funding the Hiroshima Project alone, they wondered why the central and local governments did not provide support or subsidies. They also seemed puzzled as to why people didn't donate to this project.

They congratulated me heartily when I told them that we had

"missing persons" who still lie under their feet?

That day in Nakajima, middle-school students around 14 years old were ordered to help demolish buildings from early morning, working hard in the sweltering heat. Some were laboring almost naked or wearing only thin undershirts. Suddenly, without any warning, a fiery furnace of over 5,000 degrees burned their tender bodies to ashes.

In that instant, many ordinary people around Nakajima ended their lives in a hell on earth. I want visitors to the park to remember this and walk gently, respecting and praying for the deceased.

Peace to me means *tranquility*. It means that people can live a decent and meaningful life each day in a calm, serene environment. In this state, one can perceive reality and foster enlightenment, consideration for others, social harmony and mutual support. One can learn about the true meaning of life. I think there are different ways of engaging in a peace movement.

In May 2010, I spoke and showed one of my hypocenter reconstruction films at the University of Southern California. There is a research center called the USC Shoah Foundation Institute on campus ("shoah" means massacre in Hebrew). I was told that it was a research institute to record and analyze what actually happened during the Holocaust so that people would never forget the atrocity of war and the scars it left.

I visited the center and learned that the founder of the center

Quietly Conveying the Spirit of Peace

When I hear the word "peace movement" I tend to become defensive. I attribute this to painful childhood memories connected to *Children of the Atomic Bomb*. Adults I had trusted trampled on my pure and sincere desire for peace. I felt I was betrayed. In many cases "peace movement" was in the background.

Actually, as a *hibakusha*, I would like to spend August 6th quietly mourning my lost family and offering them my heartfelt prayers. However, every year on this day, so-called "peace activists" from throughout Japan flock to Hiroshima in huge numbers, making a terrible noise all day long. On top of that, they hold a die-in demonstration and lie down by the A-Bomb Dome. The victims who rest beneath the ground must be lamenting, "For what did we become victims?"

At my family temple near the A-Bomb Dome, it is so noisy that I can hardly pray in peace. How can I join my hands in prayer while covering my ears? Honestly, the unspoken wish of the *hibakusha* is that, on this of all days, inconsiderate peace activists will stay away and leave us in peace.

Are the participants of the Peace Memorial Ceremony aware that they are stepping on the bones and ashes of countless

following the showing, a man who appeared to be an intellectual said, "Back then, Japan was governed by a militaristic regime. The dropping of the A-bomb expedited the end of the war and therefore saved many lives, didn't it?" Those who want to justify the atomic bombing often use this logic. I replied, "There can be no justifying the A-bomb. The atomic bombing itself was an inhumane crime. Regardless of the reason, as a *hibakusha*, I shall never condone it."

When my answer was interpreted, the audience burst into applause. I was deeply moved at this response in Egypt, so far away from Japan. I felt that barriers of nationality, ethnicity, race and religion do not bar acceptance of the truth as long as one speaks with courage.

I feel that it is the role and mission of those who survived the A-bomb to convey the message of Hiroshima to people of all countries. I am neither a peace activist nor an expert in the antinuclear movement. As a *hibakusha*, a citizen of Hiroshima and a documentary filmmaker, I simply make documentary films based on what I believe. And through my work, I try to persuade people in Japan and abroad that Hiroshima must never be repeated.

that the bomb's victims were mostly civilians.

A Columbia University professor asked me a difficult question. Hesitatingly, he asked, "What was the factor that differentiated those who survived from those who did not? What determined who lived and who died?"

I thought for a moment, but all I could say was, "Destiny." I thought it was about whether you were there or not on that day, at that particular moment. My mother and brother were supposed to leave Hiroshima later that morning. There were many others who happened to be at the hypocenter or happened to be outside Hiroshima.

But when I reflect, I think my answer was incorrect. After all, it was human beings that created and dropped the atomic bomb. The deaths caused by such an unjustifiable act must never be simply explained or accepted as "destiny."

Here's another anecdote. In October 2010, as a governmental "special communicator for a world without nuclear weapons," I visited Kuwait and Egypt on an overseas project undertaken by the Japan Foundation. In a region where the threat of nuclear war was lingering in the air, they welcomed me with keen interest as a "person who experienced the A-bomb." I gave lectures and showed the documentary film about the hypocenter in various places. In these countries, too, I found that most people knew very little about the atomic bomb.

One time in Cairo, during the question and answer session

restaurants, kimono shops... One after another, scenes that now live only in our hearts appeared lifelike on the screen.

When the audience saw *hibakusha* telling their stories with tears rolling down their distorted cheeks, they were breathless. The survivors spoke about Hiroshima in the aftermath of the A-bomb. The city was established as a castle town during the Edo Period and continued to flourish thereafter during the Meiji, Taisho and Showa periods. In an instant, that historic city vanished without a trace.

Today, the remains of more than 5,000 people still considered "missing" are resting beneath the park, where their bones, mostly ash, are mixed with debris.

After showing the film, I made my plea. "Because it is a symbol of peace, many people visit Peace Memorial Park in Hiroshima. I don't ask them to remove their shoes, but at least I would like visitors to know that beneath the ground they walk on lie many victims of the A-bomb. I would like them to ponder why this happened and to *feel* the scars of war, which should never happen again. I ask visitors in the park to tread gently out of respect for the victims who rest there."

Around that time, I also showed my film at Columbia University in New York as well as at the University of Southern California and California State University both in Los Angeles. The audience of mostly young students listened attentively and asked me honest questions. They were particularly struck to learn *hibakusha* residing in the United States, students and faculty from local universities, and UN staff intently watched the film that showed Hiroshima before the A-bomb in high-definition images.

Juxtaposed with the present Peace Memorial Park, scenes of traditional neighborhoods resembling the historic cities of Kyoto and Kanazawa appeared on the screen through the magic of CG. Streets lined with plaster-walled storehouses, traditional wooden houses, shops, fancy Japanese-style restaurants and inns, temples, a public bathhouse, a barber shop, movie theaters, western-style

My television interview in the Middle East

On my way back to Hiroshima, I resolved that my next project would be about Nakajima. As I was working to recreate scenes in Nakajima, I realized anew that most of the *hibakusha* who were still alive had been children back then. Many of them, too, had experienced the sudden loss of their families, the instant disappearance of their worlds. At a tender age, they were rudely thrust into a harsh new environment with no parent to love and protect them. How had they survived?

Once again, to gather information for recreating Nakajima, I threw myself into interviews. The research necessary to bring to life the five neighborhoods of Nakajima was mind-boggling, and it took me three years to complete the film. In September 2010, my painstaking efforts bore fruit in the form of *Message from Hiroshima*.

My Plea in Egypt

In May that year, a conference to review the Nuclear Non-Proliferation Treaty (NPT) took place at UN Headquarters in New York. At that conference, with the official support of the Japanese Ministry of Foreign Affairs, I was given the opportunity to make a presentation and show my film.

During the afternoon recess on the first day, representatives of nations participating in the NPT conference, UN journalists,

paper store, seafood shops, clothing stores, an optometrist, and movie theaters... There were no such stores in Sarugaku-cho, where I lived.

When my father went to a fancy Japanese restaurant in Nakajima, I used to tag along. My father, an army officer, used to frequent Nakajima with other officers and their men. I always looked forward to the sweets the proprietress would give me. I'd head back across the Aioi Bridge alone, carefully clutching the paper bag, excitedly wondering what it was—rice crackers, biscuits, confectionery candies, brown sugar candies?

Central Hiroshima: the Aioi Bridge and the Industrial Promotion Hall

exploded 600 meters above them."

The intensity of my response drew a gasp from the journalist. After a while he said, "This is the most important message of your project. People from all over the world visit the Memorial Cenotaph and the Peace Memorial Museum in the Peace Park. They need to know that it was an area bustling with activity and that people actually lived there. This is what I want you to convey."

During my flight home, that journalist's comment kept echoing in my ears. I thought, "Yes, that's what I must do."

Because of its proximity to the hypocenter and thorough obliteration, Nakajima was made into a park. As entire families in Nakajima had perished, when rebuilding the city, the government often could not find family members to confirm ownership, identify the lots, or negotiate land adjustments. Many who saw the film were unaware that so many lost their properties unfairly. They never even imagined such harsh realities.

This misconception was held by more people than one American journalist. I'm afraid many Japanese, even Hiroshima residents, believe that Nakajima was always a park. Although I cannot blame them, I cannot allow the misunderstanding to persist.

When I was a child my mother and grandmother would often take me across the river to Nakajima. Nakajima was always bustling. Toy stores, cake shops, a *geta* (clogs) store, a tea store, a

Chapter 4
Passing the Message from Hiroshima to the Next Generation

The Peace I Yearn for

"I often visit Hiroshima, and every time, I feel it was fortunate that the park was across the river from the hypocenter. If not, the disaster would have been bigger." This shocking statement was made by an American journalist during an interview after the showing of *Ground Zero—Documents of Hiroshima* in 2007 at the UN Headquarters press room in New York.

I couldn't believe my ears. "I don't think you really understand," I responded. "What is now Peace Memorial Park was called Nakajima before the bombing. It was a bustling shopping and entertainment area in the heart of town. On that day, the inhabitants were going about their lives as usual: clearing the table after breakfast, sweeping floors, doing the laundry, watering the plants, praying in front of the altar. Children were splashing in water…. It was like any other morning. The horrid atom bomb

from meaningless. Many years needed to pass before I could objectively recap the dropping of the bomb and calmly analyze the information. More than anything, I needed time to marshal the energy to face the A-bomb. It was no coincidence that I embarked on this project. It was my destiny—that's what I feel now.

needed for the project. It was a historic undertaking. Or, perhaps it was a challenge that nobody else would take on. It piled struggle upon struggle. At the same time, many people warmly supported and encouraged me. It took me a long time but finally, I was able to present my lifework on the theme of the A-bomb to the public.

The five films in the series are: *The A-Bomb Dome and the Vanished City*; *The Restoration of the Hypocenter Sarugaku-cho—The Memory of Hiroshima*; *Hiroshima Ground Zero—August 6, at the Hypocenter*; *Ground Zero—Documents of Hiroshima*; and *An Unrecognized Loss—Message from Hiroshima*.

I undertook these five works after turning sixty. When I was younger, I never imagined my lifework would tackle the A-bomb. But looking back, the fifty years of avoiding the bomb were far

My press conference in the UN Headquarters press room

Film screening at an NPT Conference at the UN

the copyright and usage royalties I could expect from television broadcasts.

Seeking corporate money was a lost cause. In Hiroshima, many companies had grown from the special procurement boom during the Pacific War, which led to the bombing of Hiroshima. Many had also profited from rebuilding Hiroshima after the war and from the economic boom during the Korean War. And yet not a single company came forward to support this project to contribute to global peace.

Here's an anecdote. A top executive of a major corporation came up to me one day at a local business community meeting and said, "You're doing a great job. If there's any way our company can support you, please let me know." I took his words seriously and visited his company one day. I explained to the person in charge the financial straits incurred by such a project. He told me that he was sorry, but supporting a work dealing with the A-bomb was not in line with their corporate policy. This was the grim reality behind the façade of the "international peace culture city."

Close friends could hardly believe my plight. "Why on earth are you so passionate about dedicating the rest of your life to this project?" My answer was always the same, "If I don't do it, *who will*?"

Fourteen years had passed since I launched the project to recreate the hypocenter. I had devoted myself to producing a series of films while procuring the astronomical investment

Industrial Promotion Center, which would provide technical support.

The academic group would comprise the Faculty of Arts and the Faculty of Information Sciences of Hiroshima City University, which was developing visual effect technology using CG images; and the Department of Architectural Engineering at the Hiroshima Institute of Technology, which was conducting research on preserving traditional towns in Japan.

For each film since this one, I have used the committee approach. Our production system evolved in tandem with the advancement of CG technology and visual effects. Collaborating with university departments specializing in CG, including topnotch U.S. universities, provided an ideal network for the production of each film in *The Hypocenter Reconstruction Series*.

In 2000, I set off with the first film in the series, *The A-Bomb Dome and the Vanished City*, for UN Headquarters in New York. The UN staff were surprised when they saw the film; their eyes were glued to the screen. For the first time, they saw the town, the houses and the shops that had stood at ground zero; the people there and how they lived. This was the beginning of my close relationship with the United Nations.

On the other hand, what always plagued me was how to procure the enormous funds needed for this project. I had to seek small subsidies from the national and local governments, and borrow additional money from the bank, speculating on

showed houses and other structures, but I had no floor plans for these houses or other detailed information. Recreating the entire neighborhood was going to be a huge project. My little company could neither cover the entire costs nor undertake it alone. Because the basic theme was to condemn the inhumanity of the A-bombing, I couldn't expect to garner private or public funds. As the survivors were growing older, I had no time to lose. I had no choice but to take out a bank loan on a personal guarantee. I had to move into action without giving it much thought.

From the response to the first film, I knew this film would have a greater impact. This would be a documentary whose meaning would not erode with time. The responsibility weighed heavily on my shoulders. I also needed more professional knowledge. I established a production committee spearheaded by my company, Knack Images Production Center, and comprising representatives of the film industry, government and academia.

The industry group would be directly involved in creating the film. My company would steer the project, supported by visionary local filmmakers, expert high-tech image creators as well as the representatives of the Yagura Group (a group of survivors from the hypocenter area), who would provide critical information and support.

The government group would comprise city organs such as the Hiroshima Peace Culture Foundation, which would collect and provide information related to the A-bomb; and the Hiroshima

surrounding neighborhood: its scenes and the daily life of the townspeople. I wanted viewers to hear them breathe, feel their warmth, sense the actual people who used to live there.

Leaving behind the afterglow of the premiere, I began my second work, *The Restoration of the Hypocenter Sarugaku-cho*. The concept of this project was to highlight how ordinary citizens viewed the dropping of the A-bomb—something I did not achieve in my previous work.

For the Sarugaku-cho Project, I had no reference material other than the area maps I had made for the previous project. Those

Premiere at NHK Hiroshima Hall

Off to UN Headquarters with *Hiroshima*

Although the A-Bomb Dome was designated as a world heritage, the original building was hardly known at all. My film was a comprehensive portrayal of the building with high-tech images based on eyewitness testimonies. It drew attention both in Japan and abroad.

Many people involved in the project attended the premiere at the Hi-Vision Hall of the NHK Hiroshima Broadcasting Station. My junior-high classmates showed up, too. When a class representative presented me with a bouquet of flowers, I was moved. They knew me during my most difficult times.

After the screening, an elderly person I didn't know came up and said, "I never thought I'd see the Industrial Promotion Hall and the nostalgic scenes of that neighborhood again. Thank you. This is a wonderful gift for me to take to the afterlife." Only one who was intimately familiar with the old town would have said this. His words gladdened me more than any other praise. The years of hard labor were worth it.

Though praise from various quarters gratified me, a sense of emptiness was growing inside. Now that I had recreated the appearance of the building that became the A-Bomb Dome, what I really wanted to portray was the "atmosphere" of the during the war. There were photographs of streets lined with houses and stores, of a woman preparing a meal in a kitchen, of a family having a meal, of a person laying out a *futon* preparing for bed, of children riding tricycles. These 16mm films vividly showed ordinary people going about their lives. I already knew that the American armed forces had a clear grasp of our city's geography, but I shuddered to see how minutely they had observed our daily lives.

There was a huge disparity in what the two countries knew about each other. The Japanese government had recklessly forced us to war against a superpower like this. What bitter disappointment must have gnawed at our forefathers who were pushed into and defeated in this futile war. America was no country for Japan to wage a war against with groundless *kamikaze* and *Yamato* spirit.

Every time I visited the U.S. I dug up more information. I visited the U.S. National Archives and Records Administration five times and the Library of Congress twice. At the National Museum of the U.S. Navy and in university libraries, too, I found numerous photographs to verify or improve the accuracy of my project. These photographs helped me confirm the testimonies and memories while clarifying the nature of the atomic bombing.

My hard work finally paid off with the completion of my very first work, a high-definition 83-minute film called *The A-Bomb Dome and the Vanished City*.

My Destiny—Hypocenter Reconstruction

demanding such cumbersome procedures.

As I continued to search for documentary photographs and footage about the A-bomb, I learned that abundant valuable material was available in the United States. *Would the country that actually dropped the A-bomb be willing to provide me with important information?*

Without expecting much, I headed for the United States. The curators of the U.S. National Archives and Records Administration, located in the suburbs of Washington D.C., warmly welcomed me. They appreciated that I had traveled all the way from Hiroshima, and painstakingly explained how and where I could find the materials I needed.

I came across files stamped "confidential" or "top secret." They contained many photographs I had never seen. Even the ones I had seen were prints from original photographs or negatives; they were sharp and clear. I procured much valuable material and gathered much information to answer my questions.

I was astonished when I found numerous photographs of Hiroshima before the A-bomb and the way the Japanese lived during the war. I was absolutely dumbstruck by the fact that the United States had collected so much information on their enemy.

I was particularly appalled to find aerial photographs of the entire city of Hiroshima. By enlarging the photographs I was able to see my house with *futon* hanging over a laundry pole. I was startled to see color films showing how Japanese people lived

My Destiny—Hypocenter Reconstruction

comprehensive picture of the ground-zero neighborhood, lost in oblivion for over half a century, began to surface. I asked resource centers, museums, archives and libraries around Japan for photographs of Hiroshima before and after the bombing to verify what we had found. However, these organizations were largely uncooperative, which made my research a harsh ordeal. For example, national institutions in Tokyo asked why I needed the material and told me that they were not able to show it to me simply upon request. I would have to go through a complicated process if I really needed it. I wondered why Japanese government institutions were so bureaucratic and unhelpful,

At the U.S. National Archives and Records Administration in the suburbs of Washington D.C.

Discovering shocking photographs at the U.S. National Archives and Records Administration invaluable stories. Despite the passage of time, they vividly remembered the neighborhood and the A-bomb as though it had all happened yesterday.

I tried to keep my interviews short. I started with casual conversation to relax them, but given the survivors' age, I kept my interviews to a maximum of 60 minutes. I told them in advance the purpose of my interview and the questions I would be asking. I assured them that they didn't have to answer questions they didn't want to. Because of the subject matter, I tried not to burden them emotionally.

Each had traumatic memories they couldn't forget. During the interview, some would fall speechless or burst into tears. I shed tears in sympathy with them; at times we had to take breaks during the interview.

Around the country, one survivor after another allowed me to film their precious testimonies. It was so painful. I often wondered if I should continue. Many had never spoken about what they had gone through. Only someone who had experienced the A-bomb could truly understand this feeling.

Eventually I was able to interview a total of 86 people. The memories of the older survivors were fading; some were hospitalized due to ill health or slipping into dementia. The clock was ticking. I feel I got to them just in time.

Based on the interviews, I examined and analyzed the details to back up the information I collected. Little by little, a

parishioners, fellow shoppers at favorite stores and barbershop pals—people would trace their memories, which would link me to someone I never expected to find. I travelled from Date (dah-teh), Hokkaido in the north, to Naha, Okinawa down south to meet and interview them.

When they laid eyes on me, the first thing they said was, "Is it really you—the Tanabe boy? You're alive! I thought your whole family died by the Hall." They would stare at me and repeat with deep emotion, "My goodness, you managed to stay alive!"

In this way I was able to meet many people and hear their

A meeting of the Hypocenter Reconstruction Film Production Committee

I decided to adhere to fundamental methods and essential principles for creating documentary films.

I searched for people who had lived or worked in the area. I tried to remember the people in our neighborhood and contacted them. Amazingly, my search turned up people I'd known as a boy. I hadn't dreamed they were still alive. Among them were people I used to call "Uncle," "Aunt," "Brother" or "Sis." When I finally met them, overwhelmed with joy and nostalgia, I exclaimed, "You're alive!"

When the Hiroshima Broadcasting Station of NHK (Japan Broadcasting Corporation) and the Chugoku Shimbun, the local daily, learned about my project, they said they wanted to cover the project and offered to support it. A nationwide search for people who remembered the hypocenter began; we were able to locate 165 people scattered around Japan, from Hokkaido in the north to Kyushu and Okinawa in the south. Seven of these had actually worked in the Industrial Promotion Hall.

I had never imagined I would be able to find so many. As my work proceeded, coverage by newspapers and television expanded nationwide. I truly felt the power of media for collecting information.

By word of mouth as well, my search for former residents and survivors began to gain momentum. Next-door neighbors, playmates, classmates, fellow students in culture classes, children's and neighborhood association members, temple

were attracting attention. I found blueprints of the Industrial Promotion Hall in an architectural magazine of the Taisho Period. With those as reference, I started to create accurate CG images of the building. I needed the scenery of the streets and houses in the vicinity. To recreate the surrounding neighborhood and its streets, I needed to map the area.

I travelled throughout Japan visiting more than 60 areas that were designated "Traditional Town Preservation Districts" in Kyoto, Nara, Kanazawa, Omihachiman, Hida-Takayama, and other places. I took more than 30,000 digital photos from various angles to use as reference. The old areas in regional cities that had escaped bombing looked much like Hiroshima before the A-bomb. These photos greatly helped me create the CG images.

It was essential that this work be based on firsthand information. Making the best use of my knowledge of the area and my memories and experiences, I took full responsibility to produce and lead the project. I searched for former residents and *hibakusha* who also knew this area. I personally met them so that I could ask detailed questions. Based on these testimonies, I developed my plot and created realistic and sophisticated CG images to visually render the contents of the testimonies.

I fit pieces of people's memories together and cross-checked them with documentary photographs and written materials to recreate *Hiroshima* as a *place* that encompassed all that existed there. My aim was to revive our lost hometown. For that purpose,

any part of the building. Why not do it? This project was an ideal final chapter in my life as a filmmaker.

I launched an unprecedented project. I would portray full views of the A-Bomb Dome when it was the Hiroshima Prefectural Industrial Promotion Hall and recreate the traditional neighborhood surrounding it.

Starting with the Hall, I explored different strategies to achieve this. I approached a company specializing in creating miniature sets and learned that a highly realistic reproduction of the building and the surrounding neighborhood would run to tens of millions of yen. That was far beyond my pocketbook. Low-level comic-type animation was not appropriate for producing sophisticated images. Architectural drawings had the advantage of precision but lacked the dynamism of three-dimensional images. I needed something more credible.

After much thought, I came across a fantastic idea. Although I did not expect much, I went to see George Lucas' *Star Wars* and I was fascinated by the robots' smooth movements. I learned that these were created with "3DCG" (three-dimensional computer graphics). Was there a way I could employ this new technology in my project? Architects were starting to use 3DCG, instead of more conventional drawings, as a new tool to make presentations.

I used connections to locate and contact the construction company whose CG images of the Kintaikyo Bridge in Iwakuni

deep in my heart years ago.

People wanted to know what the Industrial Promotion Hall looked like; its architecture; the industries it promoted; the arrangement of its exhibition space; the rooms located on each floor; what kind of work the employees were doing; who was working there; and how many people were there on that day.

I knew the answers, as I had lived right next to that Hall and spent whole days playing there. It was like a part of my home. If I had color samples, I could accurately point to the exact colors of

My home stood between the stone monument and the A-Bomb Dome.

of young people who could enjoy their lives, free of worry about food, shelter or clothing. They were lucky, living in peace, their lives unthreatened. I hoped that they could continue this way forever.

This incident, however, was the critical moment that determined the later years of my life. I could deceive myself no longer. I couldn't go back. I could no longer avoid the atomic bombing. The time had come to face it. I would do everything I could to fill in the blanks in that history. No one else could do it. On that day, I determined to devote the rest of my life to this purpose. This was the start of *The Hypocenter Reconstruction Series*.

In Search of My Lost Hometown

I found scant accurate information on the Hiroshima Prefectural Industrial Promotion Hall before the A-bomb. Particularly missing was information about its interior: the structure and facilities on each floor; the layout and detailed descriptions of each room; and particularly, the colors. The few remaining photographs were all black and white. No one seemed to know the colors of the exterior wall, the window frames, the curtains, the ceilings, the lights, the stained glass windows on the tower, the roof or the dome…. I tried to recall what I had sealed

High School Girls Who Made Peace Signs

In 1997, I turned sixty. I think it was the week of the autumnal equinox when I passed by the A-Bomb Dome after I visited my family grave. The previous year, the A-Bomb Dome had been designated a World Heritage Site and attracted attention in Japan and abroad. With extensive media coverage, tourism had significantly increased.

I saw a group of high school girls posing for pictures on their school trip. One approached me and asked me if I could take their picture. Looking through the viewfinder, I saw at the edge of the frame the place where my house used to stand, the place where my mother and younger brother slept deep beneath the ground. The next moment, the high school girls smiled brightly, made peace signs and chirped, "Yay!"

I was dumbfounded. *Do they know what happened here?* If they did, they would never have done that. They probably made peace signs when they posed at Itsukushima Shrine or the Kintaikyo Bridge. Was the A-bomb Dome just one more sightseeing spot?

What happened here on that day had already faded from people's minds.

The cheerful high school girls thanked me properly. Seeing their carefree faces, I couldn't blame them. In fact, I felt envious

principles. My community-oriented features honored the commitment to "portray people's lives from the folkloric perspective" that I had made in the South Pacific.

In *The Rediscovering Our Hometown Series,* I produced more than 500 programs aired every week over ten years, covering the five prefectures of the Chugoku Region. Starting with "A Journey to the Seto Inland Sea on Folk Art," the series included, "Traveling Rivers in the San-in and Sanyo Areas," "Visiting Seaports," "Encounters in Our Hometowns," "Wonderful Travels," "Travelogues on Literature," "Travelogues on Historical Figures" and "Visiting Artisans in Our Hometowns—Traditional Craftwork in the Chugoku Region." To the best of my ability, I tried to promote and enhance local culture.

I continued to pursue filmmaking and created many films in Hiroshima. However, I intentionally avoided the theme of the A-bomb. When people asked me why, I would simply say, "I don't want to."

However, somewhere deep inside me, I felt guilty about refusing to face the A-bomb. At some point, I began to yearn to create films that I could leave for coming generations.

was the first documentary film company in the Chugoku Region. "Knack" is not a commonly used word in Japan. I understood it as an English word meaning "skillful," "good technique" and "fine work," as in "having the knack." The word aptly expressed the kind of quality work I wanted to produce. I had chosen the name while traveling abroad.

Filmmaking skills and techniques acquired through hard work when I was a young employee of the newspaper company served as the backbone of my company. Without perseverance and the experience of my younger days, I could never have established a company.

Back then, videos were still uncommon. Even for television programs, film was the norm except for live broadcasting. I started small, so I had to handle everything myself, from planning projects to management, hiring, and even the accounts. For ten years I cut back on my sleep and worked ceaselessly. When business was bad, the newspaper company that I had worked for kindly hired me to film commercials and the like.

Orders from local companies, universities, government, and public offices gradually increased in the areas of public relations, tourism, education and medicine. I made films on regional promotion, new medical technologies, and educational films for schools and corporations. I also made films on locations abroad.

Reluctantly, I shot many television programs, but not of the superficial forgettable variety. I remained faithful to my

journalist who contributed articles to globally renowned newspapers. Still his knowledge about the atomic bombing was limited, even inaccurate.

Shocked, I had to rebut him. "With no warning, the A-bomb was dropped out of the blue one day on ordinary people who were going about their daily lives. The majority of the victims were civilians who died in an instant without even knowing what had happened. Around the hypocenter, many innocent children, old people, and women were engulfed by an inferno. The nuclear explosion emitted heat rays of more than 5,000 degrees centigrade, and together with unimaginable blast and radiation, the bomb destroyed people, houses and communities, everything. The temperature at which iron melts in a blast furnace is about 1,500 degrees centigrade. A kiln bakes pots at about 1,000 degrees. You can't imagine the heat of the A-bomb. The history, traditional culture, communities, the living environment—everything in the vicinity of ground zero was burnt to ash. Even today, many survivors of Hiroshima suffer from the aftereffects of the radiation."

After a long silence, he muttered, "I had no idea." This conversation became a remote catalyst for my hypocenter reconstruction project.

After I returned from the South Pacific, I started anew and devoted myself to filmmaking, which was what I always wanted to do. In 1975, I established Knack Images Production Center. It

I wanted to retrieve it because it was an integral part of me. The South Pacific was different from Hiroshima, but the cradle still remained there in a different way. Subconsciously, I was trying to put the lost pieces together. My journey to the South Pacific helped me regain my true self.

When I visited the South Pacific, the tourism industry was largely undeveloped, so most of the time, I rented houses in the villages. When I visited the New Hebrides' Tanna Island, known for its volcano, I stayed at a simple seaside bungalow for a few weeks. There I met an American journalist who was there on assignment. When I wasn't taking photographs, shooting film or writing stories, we often chatted. Under the starry sky south of the equator, drinking wine and whiskey mixed with rainwater, we often talked all night about our work. One night, we happened to talk about Hiroshima—a subject I didn't want brought up.

He expressed his understanding that although the A-bomb used nuclear energy, it was not different from a regular bomb except in magnitude. He said that the purpose of the bomb was to hasten the end of the war, that it had targeted Hiroshima's military facilities. He also said that while he was aware that Hiroshima was reduced to ashes, civilian casualties must have been negligible. Then he merely listed figures, such as the scale of the bomb, the number of casualties, and the extent of damage to military facilities.

He was no ordinary American. He was a knowledgeable

Chapter 3

My Destiny
Hypocenter Reconstruction

Hiroshima in My Heart

To present the results of this almost one-year journey, I held photo exhibitions titled *My Journey to the South Pacific* at the Shinjuku Kinokuniya Gallery, the Hiroshima Tenmaya Gallery and in the lobby of the Hiroshima Bank headquarters. The documentary films were repeatedly aired as a special series commemorating the launch of a commercial television station.

I spent precious time on this journey, but when I look back, I see it as an invaluable emotional journey in search of the lost Hiroshima. I had lost my family and everything to the A-bomb. The Hiroshima I had known had vanished together with its history, tradition and culture. Today's Hiroshima is not a natural extension of the lost city. The A-bomb severed the past from the present. Hiroshima was a place that cradled attachment to home; love of and pride in community; local customs and culture; long-standing history and tradition. The bombing crushed this cradle.

Men in their prime made *tikis*, traditional wooden statues of gods in the South Pacific. Sitting in the shade of the palm trees, they worked carefully and in no hurry. They had all the time in the world.

During this journey I established my methods of filmmaking and found the theme of my lifework: portraying people's lives from the folkloric perspective.

flowers were blooming everywhere. Outrigger canoes floated in the inlets of coral reefs. The traditional fishing methods intrigued me.

With Espiritu Santo as my base, I slowly began my journey around the South Pacific. From the New Hebrides, I moved to fascinating Tahiti. Filming and photographing lush natural scenes and people going about their lives, I totally lost track of time. It may sound strange, but there in the South Pacific, I was asking myself: *What is peace? Why are there wars?*

On Malekula Island of the New Hebrides, which gained independence long after my visit as the Republic of Vanuatu, I visited a seaside village. The villagers all fished together. During high tide at night, they would sink a fishing net made from the fibers of Chusan palms into inlets. The following morning at ebb tide, they would tug the net, hitting the surface of the water with sticks to chase fish into the net. The villagers would share the fish equitably. On the quiet sea, surrounded by atolls, people glided from one village to another on outriggers. Outriggers were also used to deliver the mail and goods.

I saw women make simple earthenware vessels of red clay. They would mold them into round shapes by rolling them on their kneecaps while chatting cheerfully. These were baked overnight by burning bamboo in a mounded earthen kiln. The heat of the kiln was insufficient for a hard bake, but the slightly fragile dishes were adequate for their needs.

most of the South Pacific. In those days, that area was called an "unknown world." My journey was to include the beautiful New Hebrides, Fiji, Samoa, Tonga, Tahiti and other islands where there was no sign of pollution whatsoever. Although people were not economically affluent, they lived fulfilling lives in this abundant natural environment.

Despite modern civilization fast approaching the islands and affecting the local communities, they had respected and protected their traditional culture and customs. My one-year journey to the South Pacific turned out to be a far greater experience than I had expected.

I boarded a medium-sized propeller plane in Hong Kong and headed for Port Moresby in Papua New Guinea. As we approached the equator, the view beneath me shone in vivid color: cobalt blue sea, emerald green coral reefs, pure white beaches and coconut plantations that looked like green carpets. There were no high-rise buildings or expressways. Not a single concrete structure. I was carried away, gazing endlessly at the beauty below.

Traveling from Port Moresby to Honiara in the Solomon Islands, hopping from one island to another in Melanesia on smaller propeller planes, I finally arrived at Espiritu Santo in the New Hebrides.

On small islands in the South Pacific, I was greeted by a clear blue sky and caressing sea breeze. It was breathtaking. Tropical

wanted to dedicate my entire life to the art of filmmaking.

Now I had to open a new path by myself. To spend time contemplating my life plan, I decided to travel to the unknown world beyond the equator. Pulling me was an American movie I had seen during college. The scenery in *South Pacific*, a musical directed by Joshua Logan, had moved me with its stunning beauty.

Could such an immaculate sea and beautiful islands really exist? What is life like there? How do people far from modern civilization coexist with nature? What is it like in the South Pacific, the last paradise on earth? What attracted Paul Gauguin to leave the art capital Paris for Tahiti? What was life like in Pago Pago in the American Samoa, where Somerset Maugham wrote his masterpiece *Rain*?

I decided to see with my own eyes this extraordinary world far from the material world, and capture it on my own camera. Japan had recovered from the postwar chaos and entered its long period of rapid economic growth. As a result, pollution was becoming a major issue in Japan.

I had never traveled abroad, but the support of Yoshichika Iwasa from Kure, director of the Institute of South Pacific Culture, enabled me to carefully prepare for the journey.

The places I was planning to visit were the islands of Micronesia, Melanesia and Polynesia, around the equator towards the southern hemisphere—a vast area that covered

I took a job at a newspaper company as a documentary filmmaker.

high white blood cell count. When the doctor looked at my clinical records and found out that I was from Hiroshima, he suspected a respiratory disorder due to effects of the A-bomb. Having tried hard to forget about the bomb, I was shocked.

Since then, every major life event—finding employment, getting married, having children—has been haunted by the specter of the atomic bomb.

Independent Filmmaker

In 1973, I decided to become an independent filmmaker and spend a year traveling abroad and making films. After graduating from university, I worked for 13 years for the news film department of the Chugoku Shimbun, a local newspaper company in Hiroshima. With a wife and small children to support, I was fully aware of the recklessness of leaving a steady paycheck.

With the rapid development of television, the news film department of the company had also shifted from making films to making television programs. I wanted to make films. I wasn't interested in television. Films are made painstakingly over time; television shows are consumable, transient. From the time I was 15, a third-year junior high student, I'd wanted to direct films. In pursuit of this dream, I had committed to this narrow path. I

the Department of Cinema in the College of Art of Nihon University. In those days, this was the shining gateway to becoming a professional filmmaker. Going to university required quite a large sum of money. As was the system in those days, when I reached 20, the age of adulthood, all pension inherited from my father stopped. Of course, I had no savings, so I had no choice but to support myself and pay my tuition.

One of my uncles helped me find a construction job at the Ogochi Dam in Okutama, Tokyo. I spent the first half of every week at the university in Ekoda, Nerima-ku; the latter half working at the Okutama construction site.

I had neither time nor money to go out; I just studied. Besides the core subjects for my major—cinema art theory, film production theory and film history—I elected to take literary theory, psychology, sociology, Oriental and European history, philosophy and other subjects during the first two years. I found them all extremely useful when I became a filmmaker.

During my junior year, I decided to pursue the field of documentary film where I could present my own viewpoint on current topics and social issues. Whether writing scripts, producing or directing, I decided to make documentary film my lifework.

When I was a sophomore, I caught a bad cold and developed a high fever. After two weeks in bed, I was admitted to a hospital in Tokorozawa, Saitama Prefecture. Testing showed an abnormally

Los Panchos… Of course, this was before television; little other entertainment was available. I listened to the music, spellbound.

Growing up during the war, I had known only military songs and nursery rhymes. It was all new and enchanting. Why had we fought a country that produced such beautiful music? It was so depressing to contemplate this.

Takamizu High School gave me the first hints of happiness and peace I had known since my world collapsed. It was made possible by the money from Father's military pension that came to us as a bereaved family, and other money that Grandmother sent me. But Grandmother, suffering from aftereffects of the bomb, died the autumn of my second year of senior high school. Now I was truly alone in this world.

My grandmother had become my parent. She supported us as best she could with whatever money she could scrape together. Sometimes I asked her for things I knew were impossible. After I departed and left her alone, she continued to send me whatever she could from Hiroshima. Her life was full of hardship. I have always regretted that I was an ungrateful grandson. After the bomb deprived her of any family to turn to, she struggled every day to raise me and died before I was able to do anything to make her happy. Every day I sit in front of the altar and pray for her, apologizing for not easing her final days. It is too late, but it is all I can do.

My efforts in high school were rewarded by admission to

a university that had a film studies department. I chose the latter.

In Japan, Nihon University was the only university that offered a major in film directing. The university's Cinema Department in the College of Art was difficult to get into, but I had no choice. In those days, to enter the College of Art at Nihon University, you had to take entrance examinations in three subjects: Japanese language, social studies and English. I resigned myself to low grades in science and math and concentrated hard on those three subjects for three years. I was determined to get into this university.

Going to see American movie classics and westerns from time to time helped raise my motivation to study English. I listened to the Far East Network (FEN) from Iwakuni on the radio to hear English spoken by natives. As my comprehension improved, I picked up what was going on in the world. Listening to English news, I learned interesting information about foreign countries. Even in the countryside, I could keep abreast of world events and was exposed to American culture.

Listening to music on FEN, I grew to love jazz, pops and Latin music. Japanese pop was in its post-war golden age, but these U.S. rhythms and melodies were completely different. They were buoyant and pleasant to my ears. The bouncy swing of Tommy Dorsey, Glenn Miller and Benny Goodman; the heart-warming popular ballads of Doris Day, Bing Crosby and Nat King Cole; and the irresistible Latin rhythms of Xavier Cugat, Perez Prado,

Bomb that determined the course of my life. By a twist of fate, I got involved in the production of both Shindo's *Children of Hiroshima* and Sekigawa's *Hiroshima*. Hands-on experience with filmmaking fascinated me. (For the record, if I had to rate these films, I definitely prefer Shindo's.)

"This is what I want to do. Yes, I want to be a film director." It was meeting Shindo that determined my career.

Documentary Filmmaker

In Takamizu, the distrust and emotional instability I struggled with in Hiroshima finally began to ease up. I enjoyed a fulfilling high school life. After all, this was where my mother was born and grew up; it was where my father spent his last days. The simple rustic life gently embraced me and soothed my loneliness. Those who had bullied me in elementary school now warmly greeted me.

My new life had nothing to do with the A-bomb. I didn't forget my dream of becoming a filmmaker; it only strengthened. In fact, deliverance from recent troubles gave me time to ponder my life plan.

In those days, there were two ways to become a film director: apprentice yourself to an established film director until you gained enough experience to go independent, or graduate from

bridges, I picked up the first edition of *Children of the Atomic Bomb*, the one Professor Osada handed me himself, and threw it into the trash can. Then I headed for Takamizu, where my family had evacuated. There, I enrolled in the high school where my uncle was principal. I had a heavy heart leaving my aged grandmother alone, but she strongly encouraged me to go. And that was how I left Hiroshima, the land of my ancestors, the land of the A-bomb.

Ironically, it was my experiences with *Children of the Atomic*

Children receiving *Children of the Atomic Bomb* from Professor Osada

Friendship Association decided to boycott Shindo's production.

Soon after that, a new film project started. This film was directed by Hideo Sekigawa and supported by the Japan Teachers' Union. The Friendship Association began to support this film instead of Shindo's.

I still don't know why it turned out that way. It was baffling and incomprehensible. All I can say is that we were caught in an ugly political struggle among adults. It was extremely dispiriting.

What happened to the movement whose sole aim was to aspire for peace? Even as a child, I felt a strong sense of distrust and discomfort. Inevitably I began to have doubts about the activities of the Friendship Association and the way the Osada Family was involved. I started losing interest. What's more, people who had neither contributed memoirs nor had any experience with the bomb joined the association. Our camaraderie and sense of bonding were gradually fading. I started wondering if and when I should quit.

After discussing my situation with Grandmother, I decided to leave Hiroshima. When I was a little child, the bomb had deprived me of my precious family and my world. Now I was a teen and the bomb seemed to be cornering me again. *How long is this bomb going to menace me?* I'd had enough. I was finished with anything related to the A-bomb. I wanted to cut it out of my life entirely.

I left the Friendship Association. Determined to burn my

intense loneliness. I was comforted to make friends with similar experiences. We could understand each other.

However, as my involvement went up, my grades went down, and my best friends at school drifted away. I was warned more than once by the principal and the head teacher of my grade to spend less time in the movement.

Before long, conflict developed between Director Shindo and Professor Osada over how we should support the movie production and how the story should evolve. Eventually the

The English translation of *Children of the Atomic Bomb*

A boy in high school was appointed president, and two students were made vice-presidents: a high-school girl and myself, a junior high student.

With Professor Osada and his sons' support and guidance, the Friendship Association was quite active. We held sessions to share our testimonies of the A-bomb, staged plays and chorus recitals under the theme of the bomb, and held exchange events with other peace organizations. In a way it was a movement for peace and against the A-bomb, organized by and for children.

At the frequent meetings, I met many other students who had lost parents and siblings. I felt at home with these kind and compassionate young people who had endured similar traumas. While I was with them, I could forget my lonely life with Grandmother.

Before long, word came that a movie based on *Children of the Atomic Bomb* was to be shot in Hiroshima. The Friendship Association members welcomed Director Kaneto Shindo and his staff when they came to search for shooting locations. From our children's point of view, we told them how life was before and after the bomb. We showed them the scars remaining in various places around the city. In fact, the site where my house had stood appears in the movie.

Nearly all summer during my third year of junior high school, I was involved in these activities. I realize now that I threw myself into the Friendship Association because it lessened my

The last thing I wanted to do was write about that detested experience, but an assignment from my adored teacher I had to obey.

Five years had passed since the bombing. Though burning rage and hatred filled me whenever I thought of the bomb, I was learning to control my feelings. Our social studies textbook taught us that, though nuclear energy was developed as a weapon, it could also be used for peaceful purposes to serve humanity. Perhaps I was trying to convince myself to think that way to hold back my anger.

Before long, the essay that I wrote for my teacher was published in a book. My teacher was thrilled for me. This book, edited by Professor Arata Osada of Hiroshima University, was published as a collection entitled: *Children of the Atomic Bomb: Testament of the Boys and Girls of Hiroshima.*

A gathering to commemorate the publication was held in a university lecture room. Professor Osada gave each of the 105 contributors a copy of the book. Inside the front cover were the words: *"Listen to the Voices of God's Little Children,"* along with Professor Osada's signature.

As soon as *Children of the Atomic Bomb* was published, it garnered wide attention. At Professor Osada's suggestion, a group of students who had contributed memoirs created a group called the Children of the A-Bomb Friendship Association. We ranged from elementary school students to university students.

A Fateful Encounter

A fateful encounter at age 14 would influence my life in a major way. In the spring of my second year of junior high school, a new Japanese language teacher came to our school. A fresh graduate from a teachers college, she was young, neat and beautiful. I think she was admired not only by the students but also by her fellow teachers. To this day I can still recite a certain passage she taught us from *Essays in Idleness*, a Japanese classic. Since my house was near the school, I would often chat with her after school by the stone monument in the schoolyard.

In retrospect, I probably saw my gentle mother in her. She didn't talk too much about the bomb, which made me feel easy. I only found out later that she was a *hibakusha*, too.

Naturally, Japanese became my favorite subject. I later became a humanities student because of her powerful influence. Over fifty years later I sometimes receive letters or phone calls from her. She has always followed my work. She kindly gave me an expensive imported fountain pen, which is still my pride.

One day, she told us to write an essay. She handed out good-quality writing paper, which was rare in those days; the students who had experienced the bomb had a week to write about their experiences.

their relentless pursuit of profit, often involving the citizens. They became enemies of society and the public turned against them; right after the war, however, it was these *yakuza* and villains who kept peace in the city. Back then, they were not referred to as "organized crime." I often saw *yakuza* use their might to save women and the elderly from violent thugs.

Those *yakuza* gangsters reminded me of such heroes as Shimizu no Jirocho, Kira no Nikichi or Kunisada Chuji, who, like Robin Hood in Europe, fought for the poor and weak. Today, no *yakuza* resemble them.

Though it is sad for me to repeat this, Grandmother would murmur in deep desperation, "Toshi, why don't we just go to the other world where everyone is waiting?"

I knew what that meant. I would vigorously shake my head. In those days, many overwhelmed by grief committed suicide. Others died from the aftereffects of the bomb. Many family lines ended. I was not going to let that happen to us. I would not put an end to our precious family lineage that we could trace back for many generations.

No matter what, I will survive. I will live to revive our family. A burning desire to stand on my own began to take root in my heart. Zest for life welled forth from deep within.

the war, the government of Japan had encouraged people to save money. Did banks, post offices, stockbroker companies or other financial institutions simply pocket it? Did they enrich themselves at the expense of those who sacrificed their precious lives? Solid underground safes are said to have survived the fires. No passage of time will ever clear the suspicion that inconvenient truths have been concealed.

After unprecedented destruction, reconstruction began. Construction companies in and around Hiroshima banded together to rebuild the area. Amid dire shortages of raw materials, carpenters and plasterers, prices were hiked up or unjustly charged. Many of these construction companies later grew into general contractors.

Right after the bomb, endless bouts of brutal violence broke out around black markets near stations and entertainment districts. Law and order was at an all-time low; green police officers and constables with only nightsticks as weapons would look the other way. They were completely useless in stopping crime.

In the years following the war, the city was full of lawless elements that terrorized us through bullying and violence. It was the community-spirited *yakuza* gangsters and "villains" of the land who actually maintained order.

Later, they developed into underworld organizations, repeatedly engaging in malicious crimes and gang warfare in

Boys who lost everything and became street children

with myself; in a sense a self-reflection. When I chanted a prayer to Amida Buddha, as Grandmother taught me, my heart would become curiously tranquil, and I could see light at the end of the tunnel.

In sharp contrast to the pure heart fostered by faith, the world of humans is fraught with the ugly and the foul. The decay of morals in Hiroshima in the aftermath of the bomb clearly illustrates this.

The A-bomb inflicted damage more cruel and tragic than words can express. The outpouring of sympathy and pity for Hiroshima beautified the reality and concealed immoral and fraudulent acts. Everyone should know that, in chaotic situations brought about by war or disaster, cruel, heartless people commit savage and unpardonable acts that betray our faith in innate human goodness. Many *hibakusha* remain distrustful. They cannot forget the rampant exploitation, dishonesty and foul play that turned Hiroshima into a hotbed of looting and crime. Some robbed, or simply scooped up what few belongings the *hibakusha* had after they fled the fires with the clothes on their backs. Others ransacked goods hidden by the army or civilians and sold them off in the black market for huge and unjust profits.

What happened to the savings of families whose members were all killed by the bomb? When children were the only survivors, where did the money go? What happened to assets and fortunes when there were no clear beneficiaries? During

Saikoji Temple, which was our family temple. When I sat crying in front of the cold tombstone chipped by the bomb, I thought I heard Mother and Father say, "Cry as much as you want. When you're done, stand up and go live strong. We will always be at your side protecting you."

Sometimes I stayed there until late at night, but never once did I fear the cemetery or the many spirits resting peacefully there.

Saikoji Temple displayed silk drawings of the statue of Lord Amida Buddha and the priests Shinran and Renyo. These had miraculously escaped the bomb, having been removed to the countryside one month before the bomb. Every time we visited the temple, Grandmother would tell me:

The scrolls of the holy priests were donated as a memorial by the ancestors of the Tanabe family when the main temple hall was reconstructed in the Meiji Period. Though almost everything burned in the bombing, these Buddhist paintings remained. Think of them as ancestors, for whom we must revive our family. No matter what happens, you must never do wrong.

Ever since, I have never skipped the traditional visits to the family grave and temple. Whenever I was at a loss or thwarted by difficulty, I would visit the family grave to implore our ancestors or some divine power for blessings and direction. I think that my faith in Buddhism enabled me to come face to face

doubled or even tripled. Deprived of our rights, we lamented, "If only Father was alive…"

Grandmother and I made up our mind to sell off the land allotted to us so we could build a small house in town. We finally found a humble plot where we could live in peace, just the two of us, without tiptoeing around other people.

The Truth about Post-War Hiroshima

In autumn that year, I decided to return to the elementary school attached to Hiroshima University. However, the office staff took one look at my name in the student roster and said, "You'd better give up getting back in here." Next to my name I saw the words: "Deceased from A-bomb." I had become so used to being bullied and discriminated against that I was numb. I simply thought, "What's the use?" I had no choice but to transfer to a municipal elementary school near our house.

During those years profound loneliness stalked me. My parentless state was particularly obvious at the school open house, sports day, the student art festival, class presentations for parents…. My increasingly feeble grandmother could rarely come to school. Always alone, I would grit my teeth and endure.

When I couldn't bear it any more, I would go to the cemetery where my parents' souls rested. It was near the A-Bomb Dome at

we had left was our land in the city. But taking advantage of the rumor, "Hiroshima is unfit for living," unscrupulous adults and land brokers were buying up city land for almost nothing. That was the order of the day.

An elderly woman and a child on their own were easily ignored, discriminated against and bullied. Living here and there, in fear and uncertainty, we were tossed around for two whole years.

During that time, we sometimes visited Hiroshima. In what was supposed to be uninhabitable land, shacks and crude buildings were going up, and people were gradually moving back. Green grass was spouting through the rubble. Birds and bugs were coming back.

"Whoever said nobody could live here?" We felt we'd been completely duped.

Eventually, the land we owned next to the A-bomb Dome was requisitioned and confiscated under the City Reconstruction Law. In return, the city gave us a meager plot west of the city at the foot of a mountain. Grandmother asked for a better location, but no one cared about a meek and powerless elderly woman. The officials' decision was heartless and unjust; using the lame excuse that our property deed had been lost in the fire, the plot of land they eventually gave us was only one-fourth the size of our original property. In stark contrast, property owners who were adult males in the prime of life could get their holdings

who swarmed around them. Although they were tempting, I looked the other way and accepted nothing.

In contrast to Hiroshima, "education" at the country school consisted mostly of farm work or working in the school's vegetable garden. We occasionally read textbooks but the occupation forces had ordered large blocs of "unacceptable" text blacked out with ink. We wrote Chinese characters and did arithmetic on coarse paper instead of notebooks. In the turmoil following the miserable defeat, we were not learning much at school.

Before long, it was a new year. Though I got used to country life, I was uncomfortable living with my maternal grandparents without Mother. I'm sure Grandmother felt even more uncomfortable.

We left there seeking assistance from other relatives or acquaintances, and ended up moving from one to another. My family owned many fields and forests in a farming village north of Hiroshima, but agricultural reforms were enacted that classified us as "absentee landlord." The government took all our property without compensation.

Grandmother wept bitter tears of frustration and disappointment. We were an elderly woman and a child without income; the only way to survive was to sell off the precious household items, clothing and antiques that we had managed to evacuate to a safe place. And when that money dried up, all

Life after the Bomb

Occupation army vehicles in Hiroshima

the autumn term. Most of the students were farmers' children. Since I was not, I was bullied at every turn. Though I put up a bold front and refused to be bossed, they outnumbered me, pummeled me, and made me cry.

I guess bullying is universal. When I sought help from Grandmother, she would merely chide, "Don't forget, you're your father's son." So, there was no one who would back me up.

Before long, General MacArthur and the occupation forces landed in Japan. The adults seemed jittery and uncomfortable. Demobilized soldiers especially trembled with fear.

I secretly harbored the intent to revenge Father's death. His military sword was kept in the sword rack in the guestroom as a keepsake. One day I drew it out and felt its heft. It was a fine sword. Grandmother caught me red-handed. When I said, "I want to take revenge," Grandmother laughed, but there were tears in her eyes. I'm sure she felt the same in her own way.

When deepening autumn brought the flowering of pampas grass, bellflowers and golden lace, the occupation forces began to arrive in this small village of Takamizu. They confiscated swords, guns and other arms. The village policeman warned us, "If you stash something away, you will surely be punished." Grandfather was forced to relinquish Father's military sword.

A Takamizu policeman and American soldiers came in a jeep. I glared at them, but being a child I was completely ignored. The soldiers passed out chocolate and chewing gum to the children

Chapter 2
Life after the Bomb

Hiroshima under Occupation

After Father's funeral, the blooming of *higanbana* (red spider lilies) in the fields signaled that autumn was fast approaching. To this day, we still have never conducted any funeral for Mother and my little brother. "They'll be back for sure someday," I wanted to convince myself. I still have this faint hope even after 60 years.

In light of the total devastation caused by the A-bomb, rumor had it that "no grass will grow and no humans will be able to live in Hiroshima for 75 years." Since we believed it, we couldn't return to Hiroshima. Even if we had wanted to, we had no house. Pitying us, Grandfather and Uncle said, "You can stay with us for as long as you want."

But now that Grandmother had lost her son and daughter-in-law, she couldn't stay with her daughter-in-law's parents forever. She knew that sooner or later, we would have to leave.

I began attending the elementary school in Takamizu from

the village temple. Adhering to local custom, the coffin was mounted on a two-wheeled cart and carried by procession to the crematorium. People carried long bamboo sticks with some leaves at the top and pieces of white paper attached as talismans fluttering in the wind.

The crematorium stood on a hillside behind Takamizu Middle School. In the dusk, the flames danced and swirled as Father ascended to heaven. He was 38 years old. Far in the distance, we could hear the night crows.

Rain started the next day and continued for some days. In the detached guestroom, desolation consumed Grandmother and me. In the night fog hovering over the bamboo thicket, a pallid ball of orange fire slowly drifted by. I wasn't frightened. I murmured, "Daddy, have you returned?" It was the night of the last day of the *Bon* Festival, when spirits of the ancestors were sent off with bonfires.

Of my family, only Grandmother and I were left. An indescribable fear washed over us. How could an old woman and a child live on our own?

guilt and responsibility for losing the war. Maybe he feared that his culpability as an army officer would affect his family. I still don't know. That evening, Father quietly breathed his last. His military saber lay by his pillow.

Grandfather, who had also served in the army, said, "I'll follow Tanabe." This upset and alarmed everyone.

The funeral took place two days later. As Father was too tall to fit in a regular casket, a big *sake* cask was used as his coffin. The simple ceremony was conducted by a priest called from

A *Jizo* (Buddhist bodhisattva) stands on the ground where my father spent his last days.

deliriously called out my mother's name.

Even in the village where we were staying, news about the Hiroshima bombing and a similar bomb dropped on Nagasaki began to spread. Even a child could sense that we were losing the war. Father was an army officer. I can only imagine what he was going through emotionally.

August 15th—Father Died

On August 15th, the main holiday of the *Bon* Festival (when we welcome the spirits of our ancestors), the heat was oppressive from early morning on. The adults looked sad and distressed. They said little.

When I asked Grandmother what was going on, she said that there would be an important radio announcement at noon. As our radio did not work, Father went to the house of the woman who was helping us. Eventually, he returned, supported on both sides by relatives. He seemed extremely pale, on the verge of collapse.

He lay down in the detached guestroom, refusing both liquid food and medicine. Grandmother told me that he said, "I don't see any future as a soldier. I'll go join Yaeko. Please look after Toshihiko."

As an officer of the Imperial Army, Father may have felt some

our house and in the shelters, looking for any sign of my mother and little brother.

Probably because I reunited with Father, I regained some strength. But Father couldn't eat anything and suffered terrible diarrhea. Purple spots developed under his skin, and his hair started falling out. Walking around the hypocenter for six days without eating or drinking had made him quite sick.

In the afternoon, Father said that he would walk to the Army Hospital. We all tried to stop him but he insisted, "I don't want to make your uncle come all the way here." He told me to carry a bucket and towel and follow him. As I was so happy to be with Father, I willingly did as he said.

Father took a roundabout walk along the banks of the Otoshi River in the hot sun. When I asked him why he didn't take the shady mountain path instead, he said, "Because I might collapse along the way. If I do, pour water from the river over me."

At the well-supplied Army Hospital, Father and I received good treatment. They even had new medicines. Perhaps I am alive today because of that treatment.

I think that was the day our relatives asked a neighboring farmer's daughter to come over, thinking that my grandmother needed help looking after my father. She knew how to give haircuts. After Father got a shampoo and shave, he seemed refreshed for the first time in days.

The next day, August 13th, Father could not move. He

and hands and the back of his neck were covered with cuts and bruises; he was emaciated.

Father said, "Your mother and Koro?" I burst out crying, and Father's head drooped sadly. One by one, my uncle, aunt and their family gathered around him.

Someone said, "It's a miracle you're alive. Welcome home. Somebody go fetch some water." They offered to support him, but he walked with steady steps along the cobbled path toward the entrance.

Grandfather came running. Father stood at attention, saluted and bowed deeply. "I have returned. It seems I was helpless in preventing Yaeko's death. I'm terribly sorry." Our normally stoic Grandfather had tears in his eyes. My father's manly stature at this moment had a lasting influence on my life. I determined to stay alive for the sake of my honorable father.

The morning the bomb was dropped, Father had taken refuge in a bomb shelter in Kamiya-cho, about 500 meters away from our house. The shelter covered with earth had collapsed and heavily injured a soldier accompanying him. Father carried him on his back and fled through the burning city. His body was cut and bruised by sharp pieces of wood and nails as he crawled out of the collapsed shelter.

As an army officer, Father spent the next six days working tirelessly to organize rescue and relief and to survey the damage. Late at night and early in the morning, he searched the ruins of

The End of Hiroshima

My mother, who rests in peace at the hypocenter

up those robbers." Grandmother chuckled. That was the first time I saw Grandmother smile since the bombing.

It was evening when we reached Takamizu. The loud croaking of frogs in the rice paddies contrasted starkly with the dead silence of Hiroshima. We found out that Father had called the Army Hospital in Takamizu over a military phone and had left a message that he couldn't come right away as he was on military duty.

The next day, I collapsed with a high fever. Grandmother said that she was extremely tired, too. Neither of us had much appetite. The special treat of egg soup with rice was wasted on us, as we soon vomited it. One of my uncles was the director of the Army Hospital branch in Takamizu. He came to see us. Though he gave us an injection and left medicine, the nausea and diarrhea continued. In those days nobody knew anything about an atomic bomb or the dangerous effects of residual radiation.

Just a little past noon on the 12th, I felt well enough to go outside. As I sat idly on the stone wall by the stone entrance gate, I spotted what appeared to be a military man coming toward us on the narrow path by the shrine woods. He was walking slowly, leaning on a stick. It was my father! But what had happened to him?

I ran to him and clutched him tightly. He smelled of perspiration and strong disinfectant. His head was bandaged and his short-sleeve khaki shirt was covered in dried blood. His arm

helplessness. I later heard that the burned city was quickly infested with looters and hooligans who robbed safes found on the scorched ground. Robbing the grieving, the bereaved, people without homes—this is how low human beings had fallen. Things like this amplified my hatred of the bomb.

Standing in front of the ruins of our house, we were paralyzed by anger and powerlessness. A man we knew came by saying a message on the fire cistern could be from my father.

We hurried there and found a message written on the side of the cistern with charcoal. It read: "To Yaeko: I am going to Takamizu. Please get in touch with me. Fumi (Father)." Father was alive! We decided to return to Takamizu that afternoon.

Two Fireflies

We found no trace of Mother and my little brother. They were no longer part of this world. We found out later that they had died under the rubble of our house, near where Grandmother and I had looked.

I wanted to hear Mother say, "Toshihiko (my former name), I am right here with Koro," from deep beneath the earth's surface. I felt the two fireflies we saw on the mosquito net that evening were Mother and little Brother bidding us farewell.

On the train back to Takamizu I said, "Let's ask Father to beat

Father Is Alive!

August 10th. Early in the morning, we headed back to the ruins of our house. From Yokogawa we passed through Teramachi and crossed the Aioi Bridge, turning right at the "T" over to the northern tip of Nakajima. At Nakajima-hommachi, solid structures were all reduced to ashes, including Jisenji Temple, a famous Edo Period Jodo temple; the western-style restaurant Café Brazil, and Sekaikan, a theater that showed foreign movies. Except for the reinforced concrete Fuel Hall and the front wall of the Fujii Mercantile Firm, the skyline had disappeared into barren and burnt wasteland.

When we crossed the Motoyasu Bridge and reached the site of our house, three brawny strangers were trying to make off with our stone lantern by hanging it from a shouldering pole with chains.

Grandmother was too scared to speak, but I blurted out, "What do you think you're doing? That's our stone lantern!" The one with high cheekbones grinned, came over and slugged me, hard. I fell to the ground, my nose bleeding. In no hurry, they carried away the stone lantern and then the iron bath basin.

Grandmother pulled me to my feet and wiped my bloody nose with a washcloth. I'll never forget that pain and bitter

become a river of death.

As we walked, we ran into neighbors or acquaintances. With leaden eyes, they were all desperately searching for their families. All we could do was muster a few words to try to comfort each other.

A scary rumor had it that the afternoon of the day of the bombing or the day after, many had seen a dead American POW tied to a charred utility pole in front of the sports shop at the east end of the Aioi Bridge.

It was later verified that American soldiers taken prisoner when their airplanes were shot down had been interrogated at the military police headquarters in Hiroshima. But it is still not clear why this soldier was taken to the hypocenter right after the bombing. In any case, America had bombed some of its own soldiers. Another example of the senseless tragedy of war.

Exhausted, we spent the night in the outskirts of the city with a farmer we knew. We were so grateful to take a hot bath and receive a gracious, home-cooked supper.

Finally alone, Grandmother and I took a well-deserved rest inside a mosquito net. From what we saw and felt that day and the day before, the fate of our family seemed grim. We could not speak of it.

That night, two fireflies stayed on our mosquito net.

in agony and begged for water. Children screamed and sobbed. Clusters of people lay on straw mats, alive, dead or somewhere in between. There was no medical treatment available. Girl students in the throes of death spat out blood. Old people with eyes wide open glared accusingly into space. One after another they died. Pairs of soldiers would lift them by the hands and feet and carry them to a makeshift cremation spot nearby. Heavy oil was sprayed on the piles of bodies to help them burn. Respect for human life and dignity disappeared. The dead went unmourned. Gradually, human feeling itself was deadened.

The scenes at the shelters felt unreal. I will never forget one scene, probably because the mother and her baby reminded me of my own mother and little brother. The baby sucked the mother's breast but the mother's neck dangled too low for one who was alive. I wondered how much longer that baby lived. Another young mother was cradling and singing a lullaby to her badly charred dead baby. I couldn't stop crying. *Why on earth is this happening?* Even as a child, I felt burning grief and rage.

The nearby Motoyasu River, where we kids swam from spring to autumn, was covered with dead bodies. Soldiers used hooks to haul them up and hoist them onto their boats. We couldn't bear to look at the countless children's bodies with smashed eyeballs and ruptured internal organs. Only a few days before, I was jumping with them into that river from the bridge railings, swimming to shore, catching fish and shellfish, and rowing boats. Now it had

end of the Aioi Bridge. We crossed the bridge and searched at Honkawa Elementary School. We came back towards Geibi Bank (currently Hiroshima Bank) and Sumitomo Bank (currently SMBC) in Kamiya-cho. Then we made our way east over to Fukuya Department Store. Then we headed south to Fukuromachi Elementary School, City Hall and the Red Cross Hospital. Though we thought about querying people who looked like soldiers or relief volunteers, we quickly sensed that they were in no condition to reply.

Amidst a foul stench, crowds of totally burnt people groaned

A makeshift relief station

residual radiation.

The sights I saw, the voices of lament and anguish, the intense stench, the indescribable feel of the gruesome things I touched… The recollection still nauseates and horrifies me.

Whenever I get a high fever from a cold, that hellish scene torments me. I don't want to recall it. I can never talk about it. I have never spoken of it even to my family.

Losing all sense of time, we searched the ruins of our house that day but never came across any remains of my parents or younger brother.

At night, our father's friend put us up at his house in Ushita-machi, about four kilometers northeast of the ground zero. The house was partially destroyed but narrowly escaped the fires. He suffered severe burns and did not know what had become of his family.

At the family well in the evening, we washed ourselves and drank cool, fresh water. We were so thirsty.

The next day, August 9th, I woke with a strange sense of numbness.

"I'm sure Father and the others have taken shelter somewhere and are alive." Clinging to this faint hope, we went around all day to relief stations located in the city. The "relief stations" were buildings of reinforced concrete that remained standing enough to suffice as emergency shelters.

We walked over to the Chamber of Commerce at the east

I washed my hands for a long time with water that gushed from a broken water main, I could never get rid of the haunting sensation.

We were at the center of the A-bomb explosion. I was not to know until much later that I had exposed myself to deadly

Remains of a watch store downtown

the concrete fire cistern and the manual pump at the side of our entrance gate told us where our house had stood. In the garden, the stone lantern and the stone bridge spanning the gourd-shaped pond were intact. The ground was slightly higher at around the site of the miniature hill in the garden and the storehouse, which had stood by the garden. Just in front of that was where the house had stood.

I just stood there dazed, crying, clutching my grandmother's hand. Grandmother did not cry. She stepped through the rubble to look. I could only follow her as I was too scared to be separated from her. We could still feel the heat around our feet. Only the remnants of tiles around the kitchen sink and the cast-iron pot bath told us what had existed there.

Grandmother fished out a spade missing its handle from the ruins and began digging in the area of the kitchen and the annex used as my parents' quarters. Whenever we turned over a piece of tile or metal fragment, there was a disgusting odor. I can't forget that smell. In retrospect, it was like a strong, irritating synthetic smell of an oil refinery.

Sifting through the rubble, Grandmother muttered the names of my father, my mother and my little brother. More terrifying than anything were scattered shreds of scorched human flesh. The unimaginably powerful explosion had blown the body parts of people working at the Promotion Hall all over the area. I accidentally touched some of the flesh with my hands. Though

day very clearly. I wore a straw hat and undershirt, short pants and *geta* (wooden clogs). I carried a sack containing a canteen and some rice balls. A washcloth hung from my waist. Grandmother wore an indigo top with a white splash pattern, *mompe* work pants, an air defense hood hanging from one shoulder that was crisscrossed by the strap of her canvas bag hanging from the opposite shoulder, and *jika-tabi* split-toe heavy cloth shoes with rubber soles. Though it was the peak of summer, I don't remember feeling hot.

After passing the concrete shell of Honkawa Elementary School, we finally reached the Aioi Bridge, in the center of the city. Its handrails had collapsed. My eyes locked onto a destroyed building that looked like the Industrial Promotion Hall. The familiar domed roof and general contour were unmistakable, but pitifully, most of it had collapsed. The once imposing, elegant Promotion Hall by the river was now history.

We timidly walked past the burned Fuel Hall on the corner and, next door to the left of the Promotion Hall, we came to the site of our house. I stood in disbelief; nothing was left but smoldering rubble.

The day we left for Takamizu, I had casually glanced at our house. It was a traditional thick-walled house with Kyoto-style latticed windows called *mushikomado* in the upper part and black latticework that covered the façade. No hint of that was left. Everything had burned down into a pile of rubble. Only our canvas sack with the basic household medicines, a change of clothes, and dry biscuits.

Early the next morning, August 8th, we left Takamizu on the Gantoku Line. At Iwakuni we transferred to the Sanyo Line. At each station we saw people arriving from Hiroshima on the opposite platform. I couldn't believe my eyes. Heads wrapped in bloodied bandages; skin horribly burnt a dark red. And there were so many of them. With long waits at stations, it took us more than twice the usual time to reach Hiroshima.

Just past noon we finally reached Koi Station (present Nishi-Hiroshima). Stepping out of the station, we gasped. Grandmother clenched my hand so I wouldn't get lost. Hiroshima seemed to have vanished as if by a sorcerer's wand. There was no trace left of its original shape. Structures that had once obscured the view were completely gone. Mount Hijiyama, Mount Ogonzan, Kanawa Island and Ninoshima Island looked strangely close. Only a few reinforced concrete buildings had managed to retain their original frames. The air was suffused with a charred stench. Many people were lying here and there, suffering from horrible burns and injuries.

We hurriedly walked to the center of the city. Bodies were scattered along the roadside under tin sheets; we only saw their feet sticking out. Wherever we turned, we couldn't avoid the ghastly sight of dead horses, cats and dogs. We felt like vomiting.

For some reason, I remember the clothes we were wearing that

a call from Mother or Father. It seemed like the longest day ever. Protected in the mosquito net, swaying from the cool breeze at sundown, I could only subdue my anxiety by gazing at the fireflies dancing over the rice fields. The sudden cries of a fox or a raccoon from the forest were ominous and eerie.

They should be back tomorrow....

That night, villagers who returned from Hiroshima said, "They dropped some new kind of bomb on Hiroshima. The city is totally devastated and burnt to ruins. Almost no one is still alive."

We couldn't bear to stay still. Grandmother decided to take me to Hiroshima the following morning on the first train. We stuffed

The neighborhoods across the river from the hypocenter disappeared without a trace; they became Peace Memorial Park.

inside, I'm sure, worry was devouring her.

"We just hope they will come home on an early train…."

Facing the Shinto altar in the house, Grandfather pressed his palms in earnest prayer. Candle flames flickered beside the sacred evergreens offered to the altar. Hurrying through supper, Uncle and Aunt gathered with the neighbors to discuss something.

Many times, they went to check on the telephones, only available at the village office, the post office and schools. No calls to Hiroshima were getting through. We arranged for a pick-up at the station and waited for Mother's return. When the last train arrived, she was not on it.

We would soon learn that by dusk in Hiroshima, flames had swallowed the whole city. Countless *hibakusha* were wandering, moaning in their death throes, begging for help. Screaming and crying children were looking for their parents. Phosphorus flames from victims' bodies flared between pieces of burnt and fallen rubble. Pandemonium reigned.

Early morning on August 7th began with heaviness in the air. I had no desire to play; I anxiously waited for the trains, which arrived several times a day. From the stone wall where I had seen the flash, I could see the train tracks of the Gantoku Line far below. Every time I heard the whistle blow I'd climb up on the wall to look for any sign of Mother. I waited and waited.

In the afternoon, Uncle and Aunt headed for Hiroshima to begin searching. Grandmother and I stayed back in case there was

chanting Noh verses. It was a tranquil summer morning for the people at home.

If they were listening, they might have heard the hum of the B-29 Enola Gay entering the skies over Hiroshima. The light I saw in the east was the flash of the atomic bomb. In that instant, far to the east of Takamizu in Hiroshima, a hell unprecedented in human history erupted on Earth.

Mother, with my little brother on her back, was instantly buried under our thick-walled house near the kitchen sink. At the same instant, a burning heat beyond imagination struck them. My baby brother had not even lived long enough to know what life was like in this world.

Hell on Earth

That afternoon Takamizu flew into a flurry. Grandfather returned, wiping the sweat off his brow. "It seems that something terrible happened in Hiroshima. I wonder if Tanabe (my father) is all right. Yaeko (my mother) is supposed to return today…."

He and Grandmother were anxiously discussing something, but they didn't tell us children anything. The radio had a lot of static because we were in the mountains; we couldn't hear a thing. Time passed with no news. Grandmother was acting brave but

ropes with all their might till the house collapsed. This method, shockingly primitive by today's standards, was ubiquitous.

Younger children were at home, along with housewives, the elderly and the sick. They were all beginning their usual summer morning routines. Children spread out their homework to work in the cool of morning and then bathe and play in the tubs placed in the yard or walk to the nearby river to swim or fish. Girls played with beanbags in the shade of trees, changed their dolls' clothes, or absorbed themselves in *origami*. Children could also be found playing hide-and-seek at the temple grounds or graveyards, kicking empty cans in empty lots, or playing a simple, three-cornered form of baseball.

At that time, housewives were cleaning and putting things away. With infants on their backs, they washed the dishes in the sink, or scrubbed the laundry by the side of the well. They cleaned rooms and bathrooms, hung the laundry, and aired the *futon*s. As it was wartime, some housewives, dressed in *mompe* cotton baggy work pants, would be called out for air defense practice or water-bucket relay training. Women took part in combat drills, too. Yelling, "Ay, yah!" they would thrust sharp bamboo spears into straw dolls that stood in for enemy soldiers.

The elderly would have a quick wash in the bathtub, water the garden, continue their needlework on the verandah, or babysit infants. Some prayed at the Buddhist altar; others immersed themselves in tea ceremony or flower arrangement or practiced

high-school students, were reporting to their workplaces early in the morning. High-school students were mobilized to help at munitions factories, sort or deliver mail for the post office, or assist in construction work or building demolition.

"Building demolition" actually referred to the compulsory destruction of homes by military command after families were evicted and their homes emptied. This was to prevent the spread of fire caused by the expected bombings. Grown-ups would saw through the main pillars of a wooden house, tie the beams with cords or ropes and then have high-school students pull the

Across the river from the Industrial Promotion Hall (on the left).

catching a cold, I couldn't enjoy myself. I sat on the stone wall on the side of the stone steps and happened to glance eastward.

Something glimmered beyond the valley. In the next instant, I felt a faint rumbling in the ground. *What was that?*

The other kids were all absorbed in climbing trees and were completely unfazed. Maybe they were used to such sounds because of frequent bombings in nearby Iwakuni, Kudamatsu or Tokuyama.

What follows are eye-witness accounts I heard years later from various people.

Tragic Flash of Light

It was the start of just another ordinary day in Hiroshima. The evening of the previous day, August 5th, Kure City, 30 kilometers southeast of Hiroshima had received an air strike. Since air-raid warnings had sounded through the night in Hiroshima, most people spent a hot sleepless night in air-raid shelters. The warnings were only called off at dawn. Everyone was finally released from the heightened tension. It was a beautiful cloudless day.

The 6th was Monday. Under the National Mobilization Law and so-called "voluntary labor service" of the wartime regime, all those who were able to work, from drafted engineers to mobilized

I cried and pleaded, "I want to go back with you." It was no use, but I couldn't blame my mother for feeling she couldn't handle a naughty eight-year-old and an infant by herself.

The night before leaving for Hiroshima, I got to take a bath with Mother and she gave me a thorough scrub.

"You've gotta be a good boy now, and listen to Grandpa and everybody. I'll be back on the 6th."

I nodded deeply. Though I said nothing, even my childish mind felt an odd sense of unease or foreboding. These motherly words were the last I heard from her.

The next morning, while I was still asleep, Mother left with my brother on the first train for Hiroshima. I was waiting so eagerly for her to return, she seemed to be gone forever.

In the daytime, playing helped take my mind off Mother. But when I heard *kajika* frogs croaking in the mountain stream and nightfall came with the singing of the evening cicadas, my anxiety began to surface. The eerie hoot of the owl was the last thing I needed for my loneliness. Under the mosquito net, I remember coaxing Grandmother into telling me stories to lighten my mood.

Then it was the morning of August 6th. There wasn't a cloud in the sky. "Mother is coming home today!" I couldn't wait. "Will she come back in the afternoon or the evening?" After finishing breakfast, Grandfather and Uncle got their papers and lunchboxes and went off to the school.

I climbed trees with my cousins but maybe because I was

things to the neighbors. Other than that, we just played. Kids from nearby farms joined us in hide-and-seek, kick-the-can, tag, tree climbing, swimming, fishing, and bug catching. On hot afternoons, we took naps in breezy *tatami* straw mat rooms or in the shade of the veranda. At sundown, sharing ghost stories with our cousins was exciting. It was a lot of fun; just what you would expect from outdoor summer school.

In our enlarged family, mealtimes truly bustled. Even this farming community struggled with food shortages. Breakfast consisted of tea gruel with *umeboshi* pickled plums and salted dried kelp. For dinner we would have potato gruel with cooked vegetables in broth, pickled radish and cabbage, and occasionally dried fish or pieces of chicken. If this was the regular fare, you can imagine how delicious tomato and cucumber freshly picked from the fields tasted.

We don't want anything until we win. Let's endure for the nation.

Chanting the war slogan, I put up with frugal meals like most people did. We were happy with afternoon snacks of steamed potato or corn. There were no sweet snacks like we had in Hiroshima.

It was August 3rd. Though we had just come to Takamizu, Mother said that she would return to Hiroshima with my younger brother. She must have worried about Father alone without any help.

"I'll be back very soon," she said.

Middle School (now Takamizu Gakuen) originally started as a private school called Takamizu Sonjuku in 1898. Education was based on Confucian principles and Yutaka Miyagawa, my great-grandfather, was the founder.

As the relatives we stayed with were educators, I was worried. What if we had to study all the time? But it wasn't like that at all. We were sometimes asked to help out in the fields, clean the garden or carry water for baths. Or we were asked to take some

The Industrial Promotion Hall was destroyed by the atomic bomb.

Air Raids took the lives of more than 100,000 people. On May 25th, the central district of Tokyo was bombed, and on May 29th, Yokohama was bombed. In June, Osaka and Kobe were also attacked.

At the end of June, air raids began to target small and medium-size towns. Though Hiroshima was a military center, home to the Fifth Divisional Headquarters, the Hiroshima Regiment Headquarters, and the Chugoku Military Police Headquarters, for some reason we had suffered no major air raids. Though the public may not have been fully informed about the extent of the damage inflicted on other cities, I could see that something weighed heavily on my father's mind.

Eternal Farewell to Mother

We were evacuated to Shunan City (present name), 60 kilometers west of Hiroshima, in Yamaguchi Prefecture. Called Kumage-gun Takamizu-mura in those days, it was a farming village at the southern edge of the Yashiro Basin, the only place in Honshu where hooded cranes come to visit. Mother, my one-year-old brother, Grandmother and I took steam locomotives to Takamizu Station on the Gantoku Line.

My maternal grandfather was principal at the private Takamizu Middle School and my uncle was vice-principal. Takamizu

At that time, elementary school children in the third grade and older had evacuated to schools and temples in the north of the prefecture. A bronze statue of Ninomiya Kinjiro, a symbol of diligence that stood in our schoolyard, had been removed to be melted down and used for military purposes. In addition, the swimming pool at our school was used to supply water for firefighting, so it was off limits to us.

The rice in the school lunch was full of coarse millet. The watery miso soup had just a few pieces of vegetables floating on top. As the danger grew that school buildings might be bombed, a home schooling system was introduced. Students would assemble in groups in someone's home in their neighborhood. The teacher would be there to conduct simple classes only in the morning. School was once held at my house too; all we did was read the textbooks and show each other our picture diaries. I don't remember studying much.

When summer holidays finally came, we would go out and play with our friends every day. We would catch cicadas, play hide-and-seek at the Industrial Promotion Hall, play war games in its garden, or swim in the Motoyasu River. Aside from eating lunch and taking naps, we would spend most of the day outdoors. Around the end of July, my father made our whole family evacuate to my mother's hometown.

At this time, my father also arranged for our two house servants to return to their parents' homes. On March 10th, the Tokyo

Chapter 1
The End of Hiroshima

The Summer of 1945

1945. Although Japan's defeat in the war was already quite obvious, I wonder how many people were aware of it. I was eight years old and in the second grade. My home was next door and just to the east of the Hiroshima Prefectural Industrial Promotion Hall, now known as the "A-Bomb Dome." It was near the exact hypocenter of the atomic bomb explosion.

My father was an army officer, but at home he spoke little about the war. More than six feet tall (180 centimeters), he looked good in a military uniform; to me he was a hero. Every morning the soldier on duty came with his warhorse. Father would climb into the saddle, saber hanging from his belt, and head straight for the Fifth Divisional Headquarters. Thrilled by the dignity of his bearing, I wanted to be like him when I grew up.

My father was thirty-eight years old and my mother was thirty-two. Though I am more than twice their age, I recall them just the way I last saw them.

Chapter 3
My Destiny
Hypocenter Reconstruction 68

Hiroshima in My Heart
High School Girls Who Made Peace Signs
In Search of My Lost Hometown
Off to UN Headquarters with *Hiroshima*

Chapter 4
Passing the Message from Hiroshima to the Next Generation 91

The Peace I Yearn for
My Plea in Egypt
Quietly Conveying the Spirit of Peace
A New Resolve toward the 70th Anniversary
Hiroshima and Fukushima
My Final Message
   To Everyone in the World Who Hopes for Peace

Epilogue   121

Postscript   124

CONTENTS

Foreword   5

Chapter 1
The End of Hiroshima   12

The Summer of 1945
Eternal Farewell to Mother
Tragic Flash of Light
Hell on Earth
Father Is Alive!
Two Fireflies
August 15th—Father Died

Chapter 2
Life after the Bomb   41

Hiroshima under Occupation
The Truth about Post-War Hiroshima
A Fateful Encounter
Documentary Filmmaker
Independent Filmmaker

greater fulfillment and joy than to know that young people are reading my book.

The Author
January 2012

destruction it caused. They only have a rough idea. I want them to know that people actually lived where the A-bomb exploded. I want them to feel the weight of the ordinary lives that disappeared from ground zero.

Sixty-seven years have passed. The survivors are graying; our experiences are fading. I feel more than ever that I must speak the truth of the bomb. I started to write this book in June 2011. It is based on my own experience and what I know to be facts.

It is of vital importance that the people of the world know the truth about the bomb. There has been little attempt to spread firsthand information to the world about what took place before and after the A-bomb. Many *hibakusha* have spoken about their experiences at various events in Japan and abroad, but for many years, memories of the hypocenter area were obliterated. It was impossible to answer such questions as, "What exactly was ground zero like before the bomb? What communities existed there? What was life like then?" I cannot die without filling this void.

This book carries CG images and photographs from *The Hypocenter Reconstruction Series* as well as many unpublished images and photographs. I would like to express my heartfelt appreciation to the many individuals and organizations that offered their generous support to make this book possible.

I deeply hope that this volume created in both English and Japanese will be read by many, and nothing would give me

in Japan and overseas. In the year 2000, *The A-Bomb Dome and the Vanished City*, the first film in *The Hypocenter Reconstruction Series*, was shown at UN Headquarters in New York. Based on survivor testimony and using computer graphics (CG) to depict pre-bomb street scenes, the film imparted a sense of how people had actually lived.

Screening the film at UN Headquarters and various other places, I have been busy trying to convey the truth of the A-bomb to a wider public. Through this process, I have come to realize the sad truth that most people know very little about the A-bombing. They are not aware that what is now Peace Memorial Park was one of Hiroshima's busiest quarters, home to thousands of people. I once even heard an American journalist say, "The A-bomb casualties were probably minimal because it exploded over a park." How could he not know that the park was created after the bombing?

Now, I find that in addition to conveying the facts of the A-bombing through films, there is something else I must do. I want to leave for future generations a firsthand account of what I actually saw and experienced as a child, the unforgettable truth of the A-bomb. This need has arisen from telling my *hibakusha* experience around the world.

I am compelled to convey how much was lost due to the A-bomb. Many people around the world merely perceive this bombing in terms of the scale of the explosion and the aftereffects of the A-bomb. She left me literally alone in this world. As a young boy I used to tell myself to forget about the bomb. "It's no use bemoaning our lives. To live positively, we have to give it all we've got." This approach is somewhat similar to the Buddhist path of renunciation. If not spiritual enlightenment, I was looking for inner strength.

I've long been a filmmaker, but for decades I avoided working on themes dealing with the A-bomb. I lived my life obstinately turning my back on my A-bomb experience.

My 60th birthday turned me around. I finally settled down to work on an A-bomb hypocenter recreation project, a visual reconstruction of my neighborhood before the bomb. It was a job meant for me, as a *hibakusha* (an A-bomb survivor) and a filmmaker. Born and raised at ground zero, destined to live as a *hibakusha*, I thought it was my mission to convey the reality of the atomic bombing to future generations. Though I used to hide that I was a *hibakusha*, I decided to face it and devote the rest of my life to raising awareness by making films about this wretched, unprecedented tragedy, depicting the horrific loss of life and telling of those who died in agony.

In 1996, the A-Bomb Dome was designated a World Heritage Site. To commemorate this, I began recreating on film the Hiroshima Prefectural Industrial Promotion Hall and the neighborhood that surrounded it before it was bombed. This was the first attempt of its kind, which attracted wide attention

Foreword

August 6th, 1945. The first atomic bomb ever used against humanity was dropped on Hiroshima, Japan.
I was eight and in the second grade of elementary school. Our house, where I was born, stood next door to what is now the A-Bomb Dome. Then, it was the Hiroshima Prefectural Industrial Promotion Hall. The atom bomb robbed my parents and younger brother of their lives. Unaware that it was the center of the explosion, I returned two days later, on August 8th, to what remained of our completely obliterated house. For three full days I searched for my family in relief stations set up in the city center. As a result, I was exposed to residual radioactivity and became an official "entry survivor."

The only family I had left was my elderly grandmother. My life after the bombing was hard, miserable, plagued with unexplained fever, diarrhea and general fatigue—all symptoms of radiation injury. The pain was unbearable and my grandmother would mumble, "Let's just move on to the afterworld where our family is." Even as a child I knew what that meant.

Nine years later, my grandmother finally departed for that world after suffering the misfortunes of a hard life and the

"If we cannot escape our destiny in life, the next challenge is how well we can handle it."

——The Author

Copyright ⓒ 2012 Masaaki Tanabe

Published in Japan in 2012
by Daisanbunmei-sha,Inc.
1-23-5 Shinjuku Shinjuku-ku, Tokyo

www.daisanbunmei.co.jp

Translated from the Japanese by Aruna Saito and Mukesh Khemaney
Edited by Naoko Koizumi, Elizabeth Baldwin and Steve Leeper

All rights reserved.
No part of this publication may be reproduced, stored in a retrieval system, or transmitted, in any form or by any means, without the prior permission in writing of the publisher, nor be otherwise circulated in any form of binding or cover other than that in which it is published and without a similar condition including this condition being imposed on the subsequent purchaser.

Cover design by KAZZ Creative
Page layout by Satoshi Ando

ISBN978-4-476-03313-7

Printed in Japan by TOPPAN Printing Co.,Ltd.
Bound in Japan by OGUCHI Book Binding & Printing Co.,Ltd.

「少年T」のヒロシマ
── いま伝えたい真実の叫び！ "原爆の子"から映像作家へ

2012年7月20日／初版第1刷発行

著 者	田邊雅章
発行者	大島光明
発行所	株式会社　第三文明社
	東京都新宿区新宿 1-23-5
	郵便番号　160-0022
	電話番号　03（5269）7145（営業代表）
	03（5269）7154（編集代表）
	Ｕ Ｒ Ｌ　http://www.daisanbunmei.co.jp
	振替口座　00150-3-117823
印刷所	凸版印刷株式会社
製本所	大口製本印刷株式会社

落丁・乱丁本はお取り換えいたします。ご面倒ですが、小社営業部宛お送りください。
送料は当方で負担いたします。
法律で認められた場合を除き、本書の無断複写・複製・転載を禁じます。

MASAAKI TANABE

Born at Ground Zero
Speaking the Truth from Hiroshima

Translated by Aruna Saito and Mukesh Khemaney

DAISANBUNMEI-SHA
Tokyo